SECRETS OF
THE BILLIONAIRE BOYS CLUB

CARA MILLER

Want my unreleased 5000-word story
Introducing the Billionaire Boys Club
and other free gifts from time to time?

Then join my mailing list at

http://www.caramillerbooks.com/inner-circle/

Subscribe now and read it now!

You can also follow me on Twitter and Facebook

Secrets of the Billionaire Boys Club
Copyright © 2015, Cara Miller.
All rights reserved.

"Jess won't talk to me. Not about Ryan," Kelsey said the next morning in the gym. She and Tyler had forgone their workouts to talk about Jessica's breakup with Ryan the day before.

"Jess is so stubborn," Tyler said.

"Is Ryan OK?"

"No, he's not. He left last night. He's at the condo. I don't know what to do. I don't want to make things worse, but Jess needs to know the truth."

"She's not ready to hear it," Kelsey replied.

"I can't believe the irony of this. The only reason he took Dara was because Jessica didn't want to fly back. I wish he had taken Kim. Ryan's been so quiet all summer. All he did was go to work, come home, and watch television unless we dragged him out."

"I know," Kelsey said. "This is horrible."

"Let's just wait and see what happens. Maybe Jess will be more forgiving in a couple of days," Tyler said, standing.

Kelsey looked at him doubtfully. "I don't think so."

"Yeah, me neither," Tyler replied.

After breakfast, Kelsey walked into her first class with Tyler this year. He had saved her a seat next to him, and she walked over and greeted him.

"Hey," he said.

Kelsey looked around. "Where's Ryan? I thought he was taking all the same classes we are."

"Ryan isn't coming to school," Tyler sighed.

"What?"

"I talked to him this morning. He says he's not coming back to Darrow until Jessica talks to him."

"No way," Kelsey said.

"He's still at the condo. He hasn't moved."

"Poor Ryan," Kelsey said. "We have to do something."

"I'm going to talk to him tonight."

"What are you going to say?" Kelsey asked.

"I don't know. I have no idea," Tyler replied. "How's Jess?"

"Pretending that she's moved on. She deserves an Oscar," Kelsey said.

Tyler laughed. "That sounds a bit sarcastic, Miss North."

"Jessica isn't fooling me," Kelsey said. "She can't admit that she might be wrong about Ryan, so she's refusing to talk about him."

"Jeffrey said that Dara gave an interview to an L.A. newspaper yesterday. She was coy, but later she posted herself wearing an engagement ring on Instagram," Tyler said.

"Isn't Jess paying attention? How is Dara getting engaged in L.A. when her so called fiance is locked in a condo in Seattle?" Kelsey asked.

"Jessica believes what she wants to believe. And she wants to believe that Ryan isn't right for her," Tyler mused.

"That's it exactly," Kelsey said. "She's never accepted that they're perfect for each other."

"He's so wrong that he's right," Tyler said.

Ryan was a no-show for Securities class on Friday, which was just as well, since it was the one class that Jessica had with him this semester. Jessica was still pretending that everything was fine, but Kelsey noticed that she seemed concerned when Ryan didn't arrive. She didn't say anything though, but instead paid rapt attention to the professor.

Kelsey had spent much of her Saturday reading the filings in Tyler's father's lawsuit. Tyler had given her copies when they had arrived back at school. Tyler had asked her to look for anything that would help him avoid being deposed, but Kelsey knew that the real reason he gave them to her was that Tyler knew that she was curious about the case, but wouldn't want to ask him about something so personal.

The thing that had most surprised Kelsey was that Lisa was claiming that Tyler hadn't wanted to see Chris, and that was the reason for her defiance of the visitation orders. Kelsey wondered how Tyler would react to that claim.

There was a knock on the door. Kelsey got up to answer it as Jessica sat on the sofa, reading a casebook.

"Hi, Tyler," Kelsey said, greeting him. "Come in."

Jessica didn't look up. Tyler glanced at Kelsey, then spoke to Jessica.

"Jessica, I would like you to do me a favor," he said.

Jessica looked up. "Yes, Mr. Olsen," she said curtly.

"Please talk to Ryan," he said.

"No," Jessica said, returning to her book.

Tyler sighed. "The favor is for me, Jessica," he said. "Not for Ryan."

"I don't have anything to say to him."

"You don't have to talk. Just listen."

"There's nothing I want to hear," Jessica replied.

"Not even the truth?"

"I know the truth."

"No, you don't. Not even close," Tyler replied. "I lived with him all summer. He was faithful to you."

Jessica frowned. "I don't believe you."

"Have I lied to you before?" Tyler asked.

"I don't know. Maybe," Jessica replied.

"Jess," Kelsey chastised her.

"Look, I don't want to talk to Ryan," Jessica said.

"Jessica, Ryan is a celebrity. Lies get printed about him every day," Tyler said.

"So do truths," Jessica replied. "He's done most of the things he's been accused of."

"Not this one," Tyler said. "He saw Dara twice. I was with him both times."

Jessica bit her lower lip. "I don't care," she said.

"Of course you do. He loves you," Tyler said.

"Now you're lying," Jessica replied.

"Jessica. Please just talk to him. He hasn't returned to school."

Jessica shifted uncomfortably on the sofa. "Why not?"

"Because he doesn't see the point without being with you," Tyler said.

"Well, that's just stupid," Jessica said.

"I agree. But he won't move on until you've heard what he has to say," Tyler sighed. "You don't have to take him back. But please give him a chance to make his case."

Jessica sighed and put the book on the floor. "Where is he?"

"At his condo," Tyler said. "I'll drive you. Please, Jess."

"All right. Kelsey, I want you there. I want you to hear what he has to say. And then we're done." Kelsey nodded. Jessica stood up.

"Let's go," Jessica said quietly.

Tyler opened the door of the condo with his key. He swung the door open to the darkened room, lit only by the fading Seattle sun. Ryan lay on his back in the middle of the living room floor, looking at the ceiling. He leaned his head back to see who was entering.

"Jessica!" he said, scrambling to his feet.

Kelsey looked at Ryan, who she hadn't seen since Wednesday. He hadn't shaved and looked like he hadn't slept in days. He was wearing jeans and a gray Darrow Law t-shirt. Near his bare feet, in a pile on the floor, was a set of empty energy drink and cola cans.

"Talk," Jessica snapped at him, arms crossed.

Ryan looked at Jessica, a little nervously. Kelsey felt nervous for him. It was his last chance, and everyone in the room knew it.

"I didn't do anything with Dara," Ryan said cautiously. "I went out to coffee with her before the Tactec event and then to the event itself. Tyler was with me both times. The only time I was alone with her was in my car, driving to and from Redmond."

"I saw her in your bed," Jessica said.

"Maybe, but I wasn't there," Ryan replied.

"Jess, she changed here in the condo. She took all of the pictures then. I opened the door for her," Kelsey offered.

Jessica looked at Kelsey, then at Ryan.

"How can I believe you?" Jessica asked him.

"I don't know, but I'm telling you the truth. I would never, ever hurt you," Ryan said.

Jessica looked at him. Tears glistened in the corners of her eyes.

"If she isn't seeing you, why is she saying she is?" Jessica asked.

"She wants the publicity," Ryan said. "She's making a fortune being Ryan Perkins' girlfriend."

"Why didn't you deny it to the press?" Jessica asked.

"I don't care about anyone's opinion but yours," Ryan replied. "Jessica, believe me. I've done nothing this summer but wait for you to come back to me." He took a tentative step towards her.

Tears streamed down Jessica's face. "How can I believe you?" she asked again.

"Because you love me. I love you. Nothing else matters. And you know that," Ryan replied. He walked up to her, and took her in his arms.

"Ryan…" Jessica began.

"Please don't leave me," he said, holding her tightly. "Please, Jessica, don't go." He put his head on her shoulder. "Please don't leave me," he whispered.

Jessica stood still as Ryan embraced her. Then, very slowly, she put her arms around him.

"I believe you," she said softly. "I believe that you love me."

"There's no one I love more," Ryan replied, stroking her hair.

Jessica broke away from him gently. "When was the last time you slept?" she asked him, touching his stubbly beard.

"I don't know," Ryan replied. "I don't remember."

"Lie down," Jessica said, guiding him onto the floor.

"Not unless you stay with me," he said, as they sat.

"I will," Jessica replied. Ryan stretched out and put his head in her lap and his arms around her waist. She stroked his face again.

"Why don't you two spend the night here?" Tyler said. "I'll order dinner."

Ryan looked at Jessica. "Will you stay?"

"Yes," she said, leaning down and kissing his cheek. He tightened the grip around her waist.

"I love you, Jess," he said tiredly.

"I love you, Ryan," she replied. Ryan closed his eyes and Jessica stroked his hair.

Kelsey and Tyler smiled at each other and walked out of the apartment, leaving Jessica and Ryan alone.

Forty five minutes later, Ryan was fast asleep in Jessica's lap. Tyler and Kelsey, having spent their time away talking about their Securities class, were back in the living room. Kelsey was reading on the couch, Tyler was standing at the kitchen counter, looking through a folder of take-out restaurant menus. Jessica shifted gently, trying to move Ryan from her lap to the floor. Ryan tightened his grip around her waist.

"Don't go," he said sleepily.

"I have to go to the bathroom, Ryan," Jessica giggled.

Ryan removed his hands from her waist. "Okay, but go quickly," he replied. "And come right back."

Jessica stood up and walked into the bathroom, shutting the door. Kelsey stood and gave Ryan a pillow, which he slipped under his head.

"Thank you," he said. "Both of you. Thank you."

"Don't worry. I'm going to do everything in my power to keep Jessica with you. I'm not going to let you drive me crazy about her for the rest of my life," Tyler commented.

"I would, you know," Ryan said. "Drive you crazy, that is," he added.

"Don't I know it," Tyler said, as Jessica walked back into the room.

"Ryan, come sit next to the sofa with me," Jessica said, sitting with her back against the sofa. Ryan slowly got up, and bringing the pillow, resumed his position on her lap. Jessica stroked his hair gently again.

"Jessica, you get to decide what we eat tonight," Tyler said. "There must be something you missed while you were in New York."

Jessica looked down at Ryan, who was falling asleep again. "I missed everything," she said.

"Then you can stay here next summer," Ryan said.

"And babysit you," Jessica said, stroking his face.

"I'll never speak to another girl again," Ryan said, yawning. "Except you." He opened his blue eyes and looked at her brown ones. "I missed you so much."

"Me too. I hated being away from you," Jessica added. "Tyler, let's have Mexican."

"Not Chinese?" he asked.

"I had lots of Chinese in New York. Good Mexican is much harder to come by."

"Done," Tyler said, pulling out three menus. He walked them over to

Jessica, who took one, and handed the other two to Kelsey. Kelsey flipped through them.

"What do you want?" Jessica asked Ryan.

He shook his head on her lap. "Just you," he replied.

"What have you eaten today?" she asked him.

"Nothing," he replied.

Jessica sighed. "If I'm staying here tonight, you have to eat."

"Okay," Ryan said, readjusting himself around her waist. "Just wake me up."

"Do you want to go to bed?" Jessica asked, switching her menu for Kelsey's two.

Ryan smiled. "Only with you."

Jessica laughed. "Not going to happen."

"Then I'll stay right here," Ryan replied.

"Kelsey, what do you think? Which one?" Jessica asked.

"This one in Ballard sounds really good," Kelsey said.

"Yeah, it does," Jessica replied. "Let's order from there, Tyler."

"Okay," Tyler said. "I'll pick it up. Let me know what you want."

"They don't deliver?" Jessica asked.

"This isn't New York City, Jess," Tyler replied. "I don't mind. It's not far."

"Are you sure?" Kelsey said.

"Tell me what you want," Tyler replied. The girls read their orders and Tyler noted them down.

"What about Ryan?" Jessica asked. He was fast asleep again.

"I'll order for him," Tyler said. He picked up his phone and dialed the restaurant. He placed the order and hung up. "I'll head up," he said.

"I'll come along," Kelsey said, standing.

"I'd love the company, but you don't have to," Tyler said.

"You'll probably stop somewhere to buy dessert," Kelsey commented. "I want to be there."

Tyler laughed.

"Bring back chocolate, Kelsey," Jessica said. "It's been a traumatic week," she said, gazing lovingly at Ryan.

"Let's go then," Tyler said. He and Kelsey left the condo and headed to the parking lot. Tyler drove them out of the condo and toward Elliott Avenue.

"Victory out of the jaws of defeat. I wish I knew how Ryan did it," Tyler said as he turned onto Elliott. "I couldn't believe it went as well as it did. I thought Jessica was going to kill me, and all I did was ask her to come to the condo. What do you think broke her down? The lack of sleep? The beard?"

"Everything combined, I think," Kelsey mused. "Ryan seemed so hopeless. Her heart went out to him. I think he could have said almost anything, and she would have tried to forgive him. I know I would have."

"It's so weird seeing Ryan with Jessica," Tyler said, as they drove through the light Saturday evening traffic and the sun began to set next to them. "It's like he's a different person than the one I grew up with. If Jessica only knew the power she has."

"They are both trying so hard," Kelsey agreed. "Ryan to be responsible, Jessica to be flexible."

"They'll find a middle ground. I hope," Tyler said.

"I hope Ryan keeps his promise to avoid women," Kelsey said.

Tyler laughed. "I'm not sure that's possible. I do hope he avoids Kim though. This is the second time she's thrown a wrench into his relationship with Jessica."

Kelsey looked at him in interest.

"Do you think Kim did it on purpose?" she asked.

"I'm not sure even Kim is that evil," Tyler commented. "Dara needs a lesson though."

"I'm not liking the look on your face."

"I'm just thinking, Miss North," Tyler said. "Anyway, Ryan really needs to build some trust with Jessica. This isn't the last time something like this is going to happen."

"I'm sure that's true," Kelsey said.

"Why doesn't she trust him? This isn't still about what Ryan did to you, is it?" he asked.

"No, I think it's about her. Jess' family is so traditional compared to really, all of ours. I think the freedom that Ryan represents scares her a little."

"Freedom?"

"When we stayed in the city with you two for Easter, Jess asked for permission from her Dad. And she told her parents we were staying with girls."

"Jessica is an adult," Tyler said in surprise.

"Not to her family. I think going out with Ryan is testing her boundaries, and when he screws up, Jess runs back to what she knows. And what she knows, is how to say no."

"That explains a lot," Tyler mused. "So why is she going out with him at all?"

Just because the freedom scares her, doesn't mean she doesn't want it. And of course, I think she does love him."

"I think that Jess needs to understand that Ryan and I are used to being targets. It may seem strange to her, but it's normal for us. It's the money. Ryan was named in his first lawsuit when he was three."

"Three?" Kelsey asked incredulously.

"He hit the babysitter," Tyler said. "Paternity suits, car accidents. As soon as people find out who we are and how much money our parents have, it's a free-for-all. That's why it's so hard to open up to people. At least for me. Ryan just lets Bob pay everyone off and does what he wants to, which of course, why he gets into much more trouble."

"I have a feeling Dara wouldn't have gotten close enough to you to get a photo for Instagram," Kelsey said.

"That's why I have a Kelsey," Tyler commented. "Someone I can trust."

"Maybe I'm just biding my time. Find out all of your secrets, then go to TMZ," Kelsey said.

Tyler laughed. "Tyler Olsen, billionaire, addicted to chocolate. I wouldn't pay for that information, Kels."

"I can be like Dara. Make up stuff. Who's going to know?" Kelsey said.

"You have a conscience. It's one of your best assets," Tyler said.

"Lucky for you," Kelsey said.

Tyler laughed. "Don't I know it. I'm lucky to have you."

"I'm beginning to understand why the rich marry the rich," Kelsey commented.

"You don't have to worry that they only like you for your money," Tyler replied.

"So why don't you worry about that with me?" Kelsey asked.

"Because no amount of money would have gotten you to be friends with me. You didn't like me when I met you," Tyler said.

"That's not true," Kelsey said.

"Don't lie, Kelsey," Tyler replied, glancing at her.

"Okay, you annoyed me a little when I first met you," Kelsey conceded.

"A little," Tyler teased.

"All right. A lot. But you turned out to be okay," Kelsey said.

"Thanks," Tyler said sarcastically.

"You didn't like me either," Kelsey said.

"What makes you think that?" Tyler asked in surprise.

"You almost never spoke to me," Kelsey said. "And when you did, you called me princess."

Tyler laughed. "I'm just shy."

"Hardly," Kelsey replied.

"It's true. You intimidated me."

"Right," Kelsey said, her voice dripping in sarcasm.

"You have no idea," Tyler said, driving the car over the Ballard Bridge.

Kelsey thought about this comment as Tyler turned the car left onto Leary Way.

"I'm going to go to the grocery store first. Give the restaurant a little more time to prepare the food," he said.

"Whole Foods?" Kelsey asked.

"There isn't one in Ballard."

"Too bad. I like their cupcakes."

"This store sells cupcakes too."

"It's okay then," Kelsey said.

"Glad to hear it, Princess."

Kelsey laughed. "You just won't stop," she said.

"It's my secret nickname for you," Tyler said. "That way you know it's me. Because no one else would dare to call you Princess."

"That's probably true," Kelsey agreed. Tyler drove up Leary, turned down several streets and pulled the car into the underground parking garage at the grocery store. They got out and took the elevator up to the store. It opened onto the fruit and vegetable area. As they walked through, Tyler picked up two packages of raspberries. He strode decisively through the store, as Kelsey followed him.

They ended up in front of the ice cream. Tyler glanced at Kelsey.

"What kind do you like, Miss North? We're out of peanut butter ice cream."

"I want a cupcake," Kelsey said.

"Today you can have both," Tyler replied.

"Just today?" Kelsey teased.

"Pick one," Tyler said.

"Jess likes chocolate, so let's get that," Kelsey said, taking a carton off of the shelf.

"You can get a more expensive kind," Tyler said.

Kelsey looked at the store brand she had selected, then at Tyler. "Will it taste better?"

"Possibly," Tyler replied. Kelsey took a carton of a premium brand off of the shelf.

"We'll do a taste test," she said and they walked on.

"Do you ever budget?" Kelsey asked Tyler.

"Sometimes. I negotiated a better price for my car," Tyler replied. "But I like good ice cream."

"Hmm," Kelsey said as they arrived at the bakery. They looked at the selection.

"The cupcakes are smaller," she said.

"Then we'll buy more," Tyler replied.

"I'm going to talk to your accountant," Kelsey said.

Tyler grinned at her. "Let's buy a dozen," he said, picking up a package of chocolate cupcakes. "Anything else?"

"I don't see how we'll eat all of this," Kelsey replied.

"Ryan will finish it," Tyler replied. They walked to the checkout and Tyler paid for the groceries. They headed back to the car.

"Since your ice cream was twice as much, the ice cream should taste at least twice as good," Kelsey said, placing the receipt into the paper bag that Tyler was carrying.

"Are you worried that I'll run out of money?" Tyler asked.

"I'm used to looking at the prices of things," Kelsey replied. "It's strange to me not to do so."

"I look at the price."

"But you don't care," Kelsey pointed out. "You buy whatever you like."

"I guess you have a point," Tyler said. "But honestly, I don't buy anything besides food."

Kelsey thought for a moment. "Books. *The Economist* magazine."

Tyler smiled. "Rarely," he conceded, opening the car doors.

"All right, I suppose you can have the more expensive ice cream," Kelsey said, getting into the car.

"Thank you," Tyler laughed, putting the grocery bag into the back seat, and shutting his door. He started the car and pulled back out into the street. He drove to the restaurant.

"Parking is terrible here," Kelsey said as Tyler looked for a spot.

"It's Saturday." Tyler shrugged. "Here's one. We'll walk back." He pulled into the spot and parked the car.

They got out and walked toward the restaurant, which was around the corner and almost a full block away.

"The night is perfect. Just the right temperature," Kelsey said.

"I'm going to miss this weather," Tyler agreed.

"It was a good summer," Kelsey said.

"It was," Tyler said, glancing at her. "I'm glad you didn't go to Portland."

"Me, too. I had a lot of fun hanging out with you and Ryan."

"I hope Jess will join us next summer."

"I don't think she's going to let him out of her sight," Kelsey replied.

"Probably a good idea," Tyler replied. "Do you think she'll marry him?"

Kelsey looked at Tyler in surprise. "Ryan really wants to marry Jess? He wasn't joking when he asked her?"

Tyler thought for a moment. "Ryan really loves her," he concluded.

"That isn't an answer," Kelsey replied.

"No, I guess it isn't. I don't know. I'm not really sure how Ryan feels about marriage. His own, that is," Tyler said.

"What does he think about Bob being married four times?" Kelsey asked.

"He thinks that it's excessive," Tyler replied. "Bob gets married when other people would be content to continue dating. At this point, I think Ryan's only concerned about how it's going to affect him. Whether the potential stepmother is only after Bob's money, or if she wants to have a baby with Bob that might cut into Ryan's share of Tactec."

"What is Ryan's mom like?" Kelsey asked.

"I barely know her," Tyler replied, opening the door to the restaurant. Kelsey walked in and Tyler followed her.

"Two?" The server asked.

"Take out for Tyler. I called earlier," Tyler said.

The server nodded. "Wait here." He walked to the back and retrieved three bags and the bill.

Tyler paid the bill, while Kelsey took the bags. He took the bags from her after he replaced his wallet, and they left the restaurant.

"Why did Bob get custody of Ryan?" Kelsey asked.

"Ryan's mother walked away," Tyler replied.

"She didn't want Ryan?" Kelsey said in surprise.

"Ryan remembers the day she left. It's ironic, my mother fought tooth and nail for me, and Ryan's took the money and ran," Tyler said as they walked through the late summer evening.

"How often does he see her?" Kelsey asked.

"I don't think Ryan's seen her since he was eighteen."

"You're kidding," Kelsey said.

"Bob would send him down to Palm Beach once a year, usually for a school holiday, but when Ryan turned eighteen he refused to go any more."

"Does he talk to her?"

"Maybe once a year. Frankly, I think Bob talks to her more often."

"Why would she do that? How could she just leave?" Kelsey asked.

"I think she was too young. She was twenty-one when she had Ryan. She found herself in the middle of this high-profile divorce, and she just couldn't handle everything, so she left. Anyway, that's my theory."

"What's Ryan's?"

"That she didn't love him," Tyler replied.

"That's awful," Kelsey said.

"Yeah," Tyler agreed. "I never doubted that both of my parents loved me, because they fought so bitterly over custody. Ryan didn't have that comfort."

"That's horrible. I just don't see how anyone could do that," Kelsey said as they reached the car.

"Everyone isn't like you, Kelsey," Tyler said, opening the doors. He carefully placed the food on the back seat as Kelsey got into the front. He got into the driver's seat and shut the door. He started the car, put on his seat belt and drove off, back towards Leary Way.

"No wonder he's close to your Mom," Kelsey said.

"They're best friends," Tyler said.

Kelsey glanced at him.

"And that annoys you?" she asked.

"Yes, it does," Tyler admitted.

"Why?"

"I'm jealous. Ryan has two people who let him get away with anything, and I have none."

"What do you want to get away with?" Kelsey asked him.

"I spend so much of my time trying to get out of what I don't want to do, that I'm not sure I know," Tyler replied.

"Do you really think you're going to be CEO?" Kelsey asked him.

"Yes," Tyler sighed. "My mother's already beginning to lay the groundwork."

"Is that why all of the board meetings?"

"That's part of it," Tyler agreed.

"Would it really be so bad?" Kelsey asked.

"I don't know," Tyler admitted. "It's probably better than working for Simon."

Kelsey giggled, and Tyler smiled at her.

Kelsey and Tyler returned to the condo with the food. Ryan was fast asleep in Jessica's lap. She looked up when Tyler opened the door.

"Hey," she said quietly.

"How long has he been asleep?" Kelsey asked.

"He hasn't woken up since you guys left," Jessica said. She was stroking Ryan's hair gently.

"We'll dish up food, then we can wake him up to eat," Tyler said. Jessica nodded and looked down at Ryan.

Kelsey and Tyler unpacked all of the bags and fixed plates for the four of them.

"It smells so good," Jessica said as Kelsey brought over two plates. "Ryan?" she said to him. "Ryan," she repeated a little louder.

"Hmm," Ryan said, stirring.

"Dinner time," Jessica said to him. "Tyler and Kelsey are back."

"Okay," Ryan said sleepily. He opened his eyes and looked up at Jessica.

"Hi," he said.

"Hello," Jessica said, kissing him.

Ryan sat up and ran his fingers through his hair. "Where did you guys go?" he asked as Jessica stretched her legs.

"Ballard," Tyler said, bringing over glasses and forks, which he set on the coffee table. Kelsey followed with the other two plates.

"Nice," Jessica said, taking a plate and a fork.

Kelsey sat on the sofa as Tyler went back to the kitchen and returned with a pitcher of ice water.

"There's soda in the fridge if anyone wants some," Tyler said.

"I'm fine," Kelsey said. Tyler poured water into her glass.

"I'm just starving," Jessica said, tucking into her food. "Oh, man, this is good."

Ryan smiled at her. "I missed seeing you so much," he said, surveying her with his eyes.

"Did you?" Jessica teased. She lifted a forkful of rice and beans to his mouth and he ate it. He stroked her face with his hand and looked at her silently. Jessica looked down at her plate shyly. Ryan took his own plate off of the coffee table.

"Yes. I couldn't wait for you to come back to me," he commented, before taking a bite of food.

Tyler glanced at Kelsey, who smiled. He shook his head.

Kelsey giggled. Ryan and Jess were so cute.

"Well, I'm back," Jessica said, taking another bite of food.

Ryan fell back asleep after they ate dessert, and after Jessica agreed to sleep out on the living room floor with him.

"All clothes stay on and no touching," Jessica said sternly.

"Agreed," Ryan said. "I just want to look at you."

Kelsey peeked out of her bedroom door the next morning. Ryan, who was lying on the living room floor next to Jessica and a mountain of silk pillows which Jess had placed between them, looked up.

"It's okay, Jess is almost up," he said quietly, as Jessica stirred next to him. Kelsey came out and sat cross-legged on the sofa next to them. Ryan looked at Jessica lovingly, as she opened her eyes.

"Waking up next to you was the best moment of my life," Ryan said, brushing her curly hair with his hand.

"Right," Jessica said sarcastically, but she ran her hand over his stubbly chin in affection.

"Do you want breakfast?" Ryan asked, turning to Kelsey.

"Absolutely," Kelsey replied. Ryan smiled at her and stood up.

"Did Margaret send over food?" Jessica asked, stretching.

"No," Ryan replied, walking to the kitchen.

"Are you ordering take-out?" Jessica said.

"Of course not. I'm cooking," Ryan said, taking his apron off the hook it was kept on.

"You said something about that, but I didn't think you were serious," Jessica said, tugging gently at her hair braid.

"Ryan's a great chef," Kelsey said. Ryan beamed at her, and took out a skillet.

Jessica gave Kelsey a look of doubt.

"Do you have an extra toothbrush?" Jessica asked.

"Kels, can you show Jess around?" Ryan said.

"Of course," Kelsey said. She and Jessica stood. "Come on, Jess," Kelsey led them into the master bedroom.

Jessica looked around. "Your room?"

"It was," Kelsey said, reaching into the master bathroom closet and getting a toothbrush and a towel. She handed both to Jessica.

"How was it, living here?"

"Paradise," Kelsey said.

"Particularly without your psycho roommate. What was it like living with Tyler and Ryan?"

"Surprisingly peaceful. Tyler was almost always at work, but I didn't realize that Ryan would be as quiet as he was."

"Have Ryan and Zachary made up?"

"Not to my knowledge. Ryan mentioned Zach to you?"

"He mentioned that Zach was cheating on Kim," Jessica said.

"Yeah, that wasn't a great weekend," Kelsey commented. She pulled out the top drawer of a dresser. Jessica looked inside.

"If you need something to wear, there are clothes in here."

"They thought of everything. Wait, isn't that yours?" Jessica asked.

"They told me to leave some clothes here. I think they're planning for us to stay here next summer, and every moment between then and now that we can."

"Ryan said that. I told him my father would have a coronary."

"They renovated the other bedroom. Now there are four," Kelsey

commented.

"You're okay with this? What about Tyler?"

Kelsey shrugged. "We have an understanding."

"Which is?" Jessica said.

"No idea," Kelsey said. "I'm as confused as ever."

"So nothing new then," Jessica said.

"Exactly."

"Are you still okay with this?" Jessica said. "This lack of commitment?"

Kelsey shrugged. "Honestly, I've stopped thinking about it. Tyler's going to do whatever he's going to do, and so am I. It was nice to have a place to stay this summer though."

"How's Lucas?" Jessica teased.

"Don't remind me," Kelsey said.

"Have you seen him lately?"

"I saw him in the dining hall," Kelsey replied. "We ignored each other."

"Good call," Jessica said. "I really missed you guys this summer. I might have to take Ryan up on his offer next year."

"He would be thrilled. He talked about nothing and no one, but you, while you were gone."

"It was weird, not being able to talk about him in New York. And then when I saw that girl…"

"Nothing happened."

"I can see that now. I realized it as soon as I saw Ryan yesterday. It was so easy to believe it when I was away from him, though. I had forgotten how much I love him."

"He loves you too. More than anything."

"Yeah," Jessica mused.

"I bought you a gift," Ryan said to Jessica once they were sitting on the sofa for breakfast. He placed a Cartier box in front of her.

"You're breaking my rule," Kelsey smiled at him. "No gifts over $100."

"Some rules are meant to be broken," Ryan said.

Jessica opened the signature red box. Inside was a gold bracelet. Jessica pulled it out.

"Read it," Ryan said.

"Jessica + Ryan = Love," Jessica read aloud. "Ryan, it's beautiful. Thank you," she said, putting it on her wrist.

"I missed you so much," Ryan said to her. "Don't go back to New York next summer."

"We'll see," Jessica replied.

"That was great," Jessica said after breakfast. "I'm really amazed."

"Thank you," Ryan said standing.

"What are you doing?"

"I have to clean up."

"What?"

"Diane says it's the most important task of cooking," Ryan said.

"Diane?"

"Diane Smith, author of *Learning to Cook*."

"Oh. I see," Jessica said. "I'll help."

"Okay," Ryan said happily.

"Today we're going to take a photo for Instagram," Tyler said to the girls once the kitchen was clean.

"Come into my bedroom," Ryan grinned. Jessica and Kelsey followed them into the bedroom.

Ryan took off his shirt. Jessica shyly looked away from him. Kelsey wasn't impressed. Tyler's six-pack was much better defined.

"So who's taking the photo with me?" Ryan asked, climbing into bed.

"What?" Jessica asked.

"You'll be unrecognizable," Tyler said. "It won't show your face."

"I'm not going to do it," Jessica said. Ryan sat up.

"It's got to be you or Kelsey. Otherwise, I'll have to go down to the street and hire someone," he said.

"Yuck," Jessica said.

Kelsey sighed. "I'll do it," she said.

Kelsey climbed into the bed, and covered herself with the duvet.

"Your shirt is still showing," Ryan commented.

Kelsey shifted.

"It still is," Ryan said.

Kelsey looked up and Tyler and Ryan looked her over, thoughtfully.

Kelsey read the look in their eyes. "Hang on," she said, leaving the room. Kelsey walked to the bathroom and removed her shirt and bra. She returned to the room a moment later, with only a towel covering her small chest. Jessica gasped.

"That's the spirit," Ryan grinned. He lay back and put out his arm. Kelsey carefully climbed into the bed, being careful to keep herself covered. She leaned her head on his arm, her face toward the bed. Kelsey's naked back faced the camera.

"I finally get Kelsey North into bed," Ryan teased.

"If you touch me, I'll kill you," Kelsey replied.

"Don't worry. I'll kill him first," Tyler commented.

"I appreciate your help, Miss North," Ryan replied seriously. Jessica came over and moved the towel so it couldn't be seen in the picture, and adjusted Kelsey's hair.

Ryan looked at the phone in his hand, which was positioned to take a selfie.

"How's that?" Tyler asked him.

"Perfect," Ryan said. He took the photo. "Thanks, Kelsey," he said.

Kelsey wrapped herself back into the towel that Jessica handed her, stood up and left the room as Ryan sat on the edge of the bed typing. When she returned, shirt and bra back on, Ryan showed her the Instagram post.

There was a picture of a satisfied looking Ryan, with a seemingly naked, unidentifiable blonde girl lying in his arms. The caption read:

#DaraSmith Stop pretending that you're dating me. Love, Ryan.

"Let her spin that," Ryan said, as Kelsey handed the phone back to him. He put the phone in his pocket and put his shirt back on. He reached out and fingered Jessica's curly hair.

"Okay?" he said to her.

"Okay," she replied. He kissed her hair, and the four of them left the bedroom.

"Do you want to hang out before we go back to Darrow?" Tyler asked the girls.

"Sure," Kelsey said.

"Let's go on a walk then," Ryan said.

They walked down to the waterfront, and began heading down the path leading away from downtown Seattle. Ryan and Jessica led the way, holding hands. Tyler and Kelsey followed.

"It's nice to see them back together," Tyler commented.

"I'm having trouble imagining them apart," Kelsey replied.

"Ryan would be happy to hear that," Tyler said. "Is Jess okay?"

"She is now. She realized that she made a mistake."

"An easy one to make, considering Ryan's past," Tyler commented.

"He's really trying to change, though."

"He has changed," Tyler replied. "He's completely different than he was before he met her."

"Jess said she wants to stay in Seattle next summer. She's going to think about it over this semester."

"Nothing would make Ryan happier," Tyler said. "If Jess works here next summer, it increases the chance of her staying permanently."

"Of course. She'll probably get an associate offer."

"So you need to stay here too," Tyler commented.

"Collins Nicol isn't getting rid of me yet," Kelsey smiled.

"They have a Portland office," Tyler said.

"Portland sends their intellectual property work up here. There's nothing for me to do there."

"You and Jess will have to flip for the master bedroom then," Tyler said.

"Jess can have it."

"Then you can room next to me," Tyler said.

"Perhaps. Maybe I want a different housemate," Kelsey teased.

"You won't risk it after your last roommate. Anyway, you won't ever see me if you stay, since I'm signed on for another nightmare summer with

Bill Simon."

"I can't believe that you're going through that again," Kelsey said to him.

"I learned a lot more than I did at Darrow. It was worth giving up my summer."

"I guess it doesn't matter. It's not like you'll work for him after graduation."

"True. And I'll be a better lawyer for the experience."

"How are Ryan and Zach getting along?" Kelsey asked Tyler.

"I negotiated a truce," Tyler replied. "I hope it holds for a while."

They walked along the shore, sea birds flying overhead. On their right was Olympic Sculpture Park, to their left, Myrtle Edwards Park and beyond it, the beautiful blue waters of Elliott Bay.

"How was your Law Review meeting?" Kelsey asked. It had been held yesterday morning, but in all of the drama, she hadn't asked him about it.

"Fine. Christian Brooks is no Sophia James."

"And that's good?" Kelsey asked. Sophia had worked Tyler to death last year.

"It's fantastic," Tyler replied. "He says that the Law Review will have half the number of articles that Sophia had last year. He wants to have a life, which is good for all of us."

"How's Brandon?"

"Good. He's going back to Lewis and Lindsay next summer."

"And the Tactec lawsuit?" Kelsey asked.

"It's probably going to settle," Tyler said. "Ryan told me that though, not Brandon. Legal doesn't want to spend any more on discovery, because they don't think there are enough assets to recover from the firm."

"That's good. So Brandon will have a better year."

"I think so," Tyler said. "So what did you do yesterday?"

"I read the pleadings in your father's lawsuit," Kelsey said.

"All eight billion pages?" Tyler asked.

"You weren't kidding when you said they threw in the kitchen sink," Kelsey commented.

"My mother loves litigation," Tyler said. "Her fingerprints were all over that response."

"Have you heard any more about being deposed by Chris?" Kelsey asked.

Tyler sighed. "Not yet. I really hope that he decides not to involve me. But knowing Chris, I don't see that happening."

"Have you talked to him?"

"Not lately," Tyler said.

Kelsey looked at Tyler sadly. His relationship with his father had steadily gone downhill over the past year.

Tyler read the look in Kelsey's eyes. "It's okay."

"Really?"

"No. But it doesn't matter. I have to deal with this, whether I want to or not," Tyler replied.

"Do you think your mom will settle if it goes on much longer?" Kelsey asked hopefully.

"Not a chance. She doesn't want to settle. She wants to fight," Tyler replied.

"Tactec is probably going to settle," Kelsey commented.

"Tactec is business. Chris is personal," Tyler said. "It's a matter of honor for her now. She can't let him win."

"I guess the skills that built a billion-dollar business don't always translate to creating happy relationships," Kelsey commented.

Tyler laughed. "I suppose that's true. I never thought about it that way. But you have my mother's kind of tenacity, and you're nice to be with."

"Am I?" Kelsey asked. Tyler smiled at her.

"You know you are," he replied.

Kelsey glanced ahead of her. Ryan and Jessica were softly talking to each other, Ryan's arm around Jessica's waist.

"I haven't created a billion-dollar company, though." Kelsey said.

"Do you want to?" Tyler asked.

"I don't know. Maybe."

"You have plenty of time. My mother was older than you are now when she started Tactec," Tyler replied.

"How did she come up with the idea?" Kelsey asked.

"She met Bob and they went to went to happy hour after work one night. They came up with the business plan on a cocktail napkin, quit their jobs the next week, and started the company less than a month later."

"Seriously?"

"My mother says that Chris went ballistic."

"You were a baby?"

"I was. I don't remember Mom working on anything other than Tactec," Tyler said.

"The risk certainly paid off."

"For my mother. For Chris, not so much," Tyler said.

"Do you think that's why he filed suit?" Kelsey asked.

"It's all about the money for him now," Tyler replied.

"Isn't his gallery doing well?" Kelsey asked.

"Not as well as Tactec."

"Well, of course not."

"I really think that bothers him."

"He sells wood sculptures, not technology. One is certainly more profitable than the other," Kelsey commented.

"Chris doesn't want to admit that Lisa is smarter than he is. It upsets him," Tyler replied.

"Why? Wasn't she his lawyer?"

"She was. I don't know what Chris's problem is. I just wish he'd work it out in therapy instead of dragging all of us into court."

Kelsey glanced at Tyler, and at the water behind him. Ryan turned around.

"Should we head back?" he asked. Kelsey looked up. Ahead of them in the distance was the grain terminal. A bike zipped past them on the bike path.

Tyler shook his head. "Not yet. It's a beautiful day."

Ryan looked at Jessica. "To be with beautiful girls." Jessica smiled at him.

Tyler looked at Kelsey. His brown eyes shined. "Absolutely."

Kelsey blushed.

Second and third year at Darrow was organized very differently than first year. Instead of large classes, small seminar groups of between five and twenty students were the norm. Unlike first year, second and third year classes were not graded on a curve, so it was possible for the entire class to get A's. Of course it was also possible for the entire class to get C's. So there was only a little comfort in the new grading structure.

Darrow was also slightly different than other elite law schools in that instead of taking a random variety of classes, students chose one of ten tracks of classes.

Kelsey and Tyler took the Intellectual Property track, and Ryan, who fully intended to continue to use Tyler's outlines, joined them. Jessica and Zachary both decided to focus on the Financial Law track, which would lead to learning about Mergers, Acquisitions, and Tax.

The tracks overlapped in various classes, so Kelsey and Jessica were taking Securities together now and would take Negotiation classes together later this year.

On Monday, Kelsey and Jessica joined the boys for lunch. It was Tyler's birthday, and they would have a party for him in the evening.

Jeffrey walked into the dining hall, and up to the table. Tyler looked up at him, quizzically.

"Happy birthday, Tyler," Jeffrey said.

"Thanks," Tyler replied. "Why are you here now? Aren't you and Mariel coming later this afternoon?"

"Your mother asked me to deliver your gift to you."

Tyler looked at him in interest.

"Really? Why?" Tyler asked. Jeffrey didn't answer, but handed Tyler an envelope. Tyler opened it as Ryan looked over his shoulder. Tyler removed a ordinary birthday card from the envelope. He opened it, and a check was inside. Ryan snatched the check out of the card and looked at it.

"Wow," Ryan said impressed, but Tyler paid no attention to him. Instead he burst out laughing.

"Don't spend it yet, Ryan," Tyler said, handing him the card. Ryan took the card, read it and smiled.

"I love Lisa," Ryan said, shaking his head.

"What does it say?" Jessica asked.

"Read it out loud," Tyler said to Ryan.

"Happy birthday, Tyler. Whatever you don't spend on legal expenses is your birthday gift. Don't let the idiot who contributed your Y chromosome depose you. Love, Mom," Ryan read. Kelsey saw Jeffrey try and fail to suppress a smile.

Tyler handed the check back to Jeffrey. "Please deposit it into my usual account," Tyler said.

Jeffrey took the check and put it into the breast pocket of his suit. "Will do," he said. "Mariel and I will be back at two."

"Okay. Thanks for bringing the card," Tyler said.

"You're welcome. Have a nice birthday, Tyler," Jeffrey said. And he left the dining hall.

Tyler looked at Ryan and laughed.

"It's going to be a great year," he commented.

"Make sure you buy Tyler a gift," Kelsey said to Zachary after lunch. Tyler had run over to the Law Review offices, and Ryan and Jessica were walking ahead of them, hand in hand.

"What?" Zach said. "I'm not buying Tyler a gift. Do you know how much money he has?"

"Zachary. I can't believe you call yourself a friend and you can't spend ten bucks on a token present," Kelsey said.

"He doesn't need it."

"Kim didn't need three-thousand-dollar earrings," Kelsey pointed out.

"Three thousand, three hundred. But who's counting?" Zach said.

"Exactly. Don't come empty-handed. Otherwise, I won't let you have any cake," Kelsey said.

"Yes, Ma'am," Zach said with sarcasm.

"I mean it," Kelsey said.

"Fine," Zach said.

"This is nice, Ryan. You too, Jess. Thank you," Tyler said that evening at dinner. Ryan smiled at him, as he put a plate of channa masala onto the table.

"You're welcome," Ryan said.

"Happy birthday, Tyler," Jessica said.

"I can't believe you made all of this," Zach said. "I'm impressed."

"It looks delicious, you guys," Kelsey said.

"Thanks, Kels," Jessica said. "Ryan did most of the work though."

"You helped."

"I washed dishes," Jessica said.

"That's helping," Ryan commented. "So should we sing 'Happy Birthday' to you?

Tyler caught Kelsey's eye and they laughed.

"What?" Zach asked.

"Ryan wasn't in Copyright class the first day. It turns out that there's a big class action lawsuit about the rights to using the song," Tyler said.

"But we can sing it to Tyler," Kelsey said.

"Do we have to pay a licensing fee?" Jessica asked seriously.

"No," Kelsey laughed.

After Ryan's Indian feast, Tyler opened his gifts.

Tyler unwrapped Kelsey's gift first. It was a green book, with a gilt title. Tyler's eyes widened as he picked it up and examined it. He opened the book and looked at the title page.

"Kelsey, thank you," Tyler said.

"What is it?" Jessica asked.

"A book by Clarence Darrow, about his childhood," Tyler said, handing the book gently to Jessica.

"Our Darrow?" Jessica said, opening the book. "It's a first edition," she said in surprise.

Zach looked at Kelsey.

"Did someone recently become a heiress?" he asked. Kelsey just smiled. The book had cost less than fifty dollars. She had found Tyler's copy online.

Jessica passed the book to Ryan, who glanced through it. "Nice one, Kels," he said, handing the book back to Tyler.

"Now my gift is going to look cheap," Zach commented.

"You bought me a gift?" Tyler asked Zach.

"Kelsey said I had to," Zach pouted.

"Wow. A gift from Zachary Payne. This is a red-letter day," Tyler teased. "Give it."

Zachary frowned at Kelsey and handed Tyler a large gift bag.

"It better be good," Kelsey whispered to him. "Or no cake."

"It's fabulous," Zach whispered back. He looked at Tyler as Tyler opened it.

Tyler pulled a navy twill briefcase out of the gift bag.

"Thank you, Zach," Tyler said.

"It's Filson," Zach commented.

"I can see. Keep your hands off of it, Ryan," Tyler warned.

Ryan pouted.

"It's really nice," Jessica said. She reached out and took it from Tyler, running her finger over the leather strap.

"It is. Good job, Zach," Kelsey said.

"The things I do for cake," Zach commented. Kelsey giggled.

Kelsey loved their new home. Instead of the cramped dorm room that they had shared on campus, she and Jessica now had a beautiful two-bedroom apartment with a small kitchen and bath. The first thing that Kelsey had noticed when she had walked in was that the apartment had been substantially upgraded since they had seen it with the boys last spring. It took a few days before she had realized that the upgrades had been arranged by Jeffrey and not by the actual landlord.

The first thing she had noticed was the lightning-fast wifi that had been installed. Kelsey was expecting the slow-but-serviceable internet that they had had in the dorms, but instead she discovered that something that took two minutes to download in her former room, took mere seconds in the new apartment.

They had also been provided with brand new, flat-screen televisions in both bedrooms, as well as the living room. Each television had full cable, with more channels than Kelsey cared to count. The kitchen had been upgraded with several appliances, including an automatic hot water heater, water filter, and a brand new refrigerator. The living room had brand new furniture, and the bedrooms had new mattresses and beautiful, soft bedding.

She and Jessica had declined to have Mariel clean for them twice per week, although Mariel continued to clean for the boys. So instead the apartment had been stocked with a full range of cleaning supplies, including a state of the art Dyson vacuum.

To Kelsey's amusement, Jeffrey had also placed six boxes of Kelsey's favorite hot chocolate packets in the cabinet, as well as her preferred green tea. She knew if she asked, Jeffrey would say it was for when the boys came over to visit.

Despite all of the upgrades and changes, Kelsey and Jessica had been told by Jeffrey that they would be expected to pay him the amount that they had agreed upon last spring. Jeffrey would pay the landlord for both apartments.

One thing that had surprised Kelsey was that she and Jessica had been given keys to the boys' apartment. When Kelsey had asked Jeffrey, he commented that both Ryan and Tyler had requested that the girls be given keys and that even Zach thought it was a good idea, so he wouldn't have to answer the door. Jessica declined to give the boys a key to the girls' apartment.

"I want to be able to sit around in my jammies." she had told Jeffrey. But as Kelsey knew, the real reason was that Jessica didn't want any surprise visits from Ryan.

"Who knows what he'd do?" Jessica had said to Kelsey.

"Probably nothing," Kelsey had commented.

"I'm not risking it," Jessica had said.

Kelsey was working on Securities with Tyler in the boys' apartment. Ryan and Zach were sitting watching the Mariners game on television.

"Hey, Tyler. It looks like your mom is still dating Tim Mayer," Zach said.

Ryan snickered as Tyler and Kelsey looked up and saw the television screen. On the Jumbotron, Lisa and Tim were sitting in the stands kissing, and the caption under them read, *Tactec CEO Lisa Olsen and guest.*

"Seems so," Tyler commented, looking back at his work.

First thing in the morning, Kelsey saw Tyler at the apartment gym. Per usual, he arrived a few minutes after she did, worked on the elliptical machine and did weights. Unlike last year, he usually said a few words to her, although still not very many. Tyler wasn't a morning person.

Next, she usually sat with Tyler and Ryan at breakfast. Jessica and Zachary had both decided to take late morning classes, so they usually slept through breakfast.

Then Kelsey, Tyler, and Ryan would head to class together, or walk back over to the apartment.

Usually, Jess and Zach would join the trio for lunch.

In the afternoon, Tyler would usually walk over to the Law Review offices. Kelsey and Jess usually ended up studying in their apartment with Ryan. But then everyone would regroup for dinner on campus, unless Ryan cooked for Jess, then it was just Kelsey, Tyler and Zach. Occasionally one of their classmates would make a cameo appearance at dinner, but Darrow had a small student body, and the students had formed cliques pretty quickly.

Throughout the day they would talk about class, or law review, or life, and Jeffrey would occasionally drop by with mail, folders or documents for Tyler to sign. Unlike last year, Jeffrey was a much more common presence. Kelsey thought it was because of the constant board meetings that Lisa had excused Tyler from for the semester, but that he was still expected to keep track of. Tyler's life was a whirlwind, but he always made time for her. Except of course, in the way she wanted, by asking her out on a date.

"Tyler," Professor Buxton said as Tyler, Zach and Kelsey were walking out of the classroom.

"Professor?" Tyler asked, stopping. Kelsey and Zach stopped as well.

"Dean Wilson would like to see you. Drop by his office sometime today," the Professor said.

"Okay. Thank you," Tyler said. They walked out of the room.

"No time like the present," Tyler said. "I'll see you guys at lunch."

"Okay," Kelsey said. She waved at him and he turned toward the administration building while she walked to lunch with Zach.

An hour later, Kelsey, Zachary, Ryan, and Jessica were walking to the apartment building. Tyler hadn't shown up, and Zachary suggested that they head back.

"Do you want to study with us?" Jessica asked Ryan, as they walked into the building. Zachary pushed the elevator button.

"Of course," Ryan said happily. The group went upstairs.

"See you later," Zachary said, pulling out his keys.

"Join us," Kelsey said to him.

"Study?" Zach said doubtfully.

"You need to," Ryan commented.

"Shut up. I don't need to hear that from you," Zachary said.

"I don't know who else will tell you. Tyler's going to watch you fail out, because he doesn't want to irritate you," Ryan said.

"Fine. I'll be over in a minute," Zachary said. "I don't want you to do better than me for a third semester." Zach opened the door to the boys' apartment and went inside, while Ryan, Kelsey, and Jessica went to the girls' apartment. Ryan sat on the sofa, while Kelsey put her backpack into her room.

"Do you want tea?" Jessica asked Ryan.

"Sure," Ryan said, taking out his iPad.

Kelsey returned to the living room.

"Tea, Kels?"

"Thanks, Jess. Mint, please," Kelsey replied.

There was a knock on the door, then Zachary and Tyler walked into the apartment.

"There you are," Ryan said. "Why didn't you come to lunch?"

"Dean Wilson took longer than I expected," Tyler replied. He sat on the sofa next to Ryan.

"Do you guys want tea?" Jessica asked.

"No, thanks," Zachary said.

"Do you have food?" Tyler asked.

"Absolutely," Jessica replied.

"I'll get you some," Kelsey said heading to the kitchen.

"Thanks," Tyler said.

"I'll help," Ryan said, scrambling to his feet to help Jessica with the tea cups.

Ryan, Jessica, and Kelsey assembled tea cups and snacks while Zachary looked at his phone messages and Tyler looked at the ceiling.

"Eat," Kelsey said, placing a plate of scones in front of Tyler. Tyler grinned at her and she smiled back. Ryan had made them.

"Blueberry. Thanks, Kels. And Ryan."

"You're welcome," Ryan said. He carried over two steaming mugs and placed them on the table. Then he sat cross-legged on the floor. Jessica and Kelsey joined them, carrying mugs of their own. Jessica sat next to Ryan, while Kelsey took the chair.

"So what did the dean want?" Zachary asked Tyler, putting his phone away.

Tyler sighed. "Moot court is coming up," he began. Kelsey nodded thoughtfully. Moot court would be held the week before Thanksgiving and they would be re-partnered with their Legal Writing partners, which meant that Kelsey and Tyler would be working on it together.

"Unlike most law schools, Darrow always uses a family law and a criminal law case for moot court. It turns out that for the past seven years, Darrow has used a variation of my parents' visitation fight for moot court."

"You're kidding," Jessica said, taking a sip of her tea. Tyler broke off a piece of scone and ate it.

"Dean Wilson said that I could choose whether I wanted to work on the visitation hypothetical or not. Everyone else except for Alana Alexander is going to be assigned a case. She and her partner can decide as well."

"Why Alana?" Kelsey asked.

"Alana's father was a prosecutor who was assassinated while working on a drug case. That's the criminal law hypothetical for moot court this year."

"Wow," Jessica said, sipping her tea.

"So Kels, you and I need to decide which to take. Dean Wilson wants us to work on the no-visitation side if we take it, though."

"He figures you know a thousand arguments for the benefit of visitation?" Zachary asked, taking a scone. Ryan glanced at him.

"Exactly," Tyler said.

"You should do the drug case," Ryan said.

"Definitely," Zachary said.

"Actually, I was leaning toward doing the visitation case," Tyler said thoughtfully.

"This isn't therapy," Zach said.

"It's not graded," Tyler said.

"Does Dean Wilson know your parents are suing each other over this right now?" Zachary asked.

"I told him," Tyler said, eating another piece of scone.

"You're crazy if you do visitation," Zach said.

"Perhaps I'd understand my parents better. Dean Wilson did say that there are some significant fact changes in the hypothetical, so it won't be exactly the same."

"I agree with Zach. Don't do it," Jessica said.

"What do you think, Kelsey?"

Kelsey thought for a moment. Honestly, she really didn't want to work on a drug case. Although she had enjoyed criminal law class, she wasn't sure that she would be comfortable either prosecuting or defending a drug dealer. Somehow it felt like it hit a little close to home.

"It's up to you," Kelsey said. Tyler looked at her in interest.

"You don't have an opinion? You have to work on it too," Ryan said.

"It's Tyler's life. I think he should decide," Kelsey said.

"Don't do it, Tyler," Zach said.

"If Kelsey doesn't care, I'll think about it," Tyler said, finishing the scone.

"Chris will be here next week, you can ask him what he thinks," Ryan

commented.

"Your Dad's coming to Seattle?" Jessica asked.

"Yes," Tyler said.

"You should take Kelsey," Zach said.

"Kelsey doesn't want to go," Tyler said.

"How do you know, Tyler? You haven't asked me," Kelsey replied.

"He hasn't asked you anything," Ryan commented.

"Shut up, Ryan," Tyler said. "Okay, Kelsey. Would you like to watch my father and me fight about his lawsuit over dinner?"

"Where are you going?" Kelsey teased.

"It doesn't matter. You have to go, since you mentioned that I hadn't asked you."

"I'll go," Kelsey smiled.

"Don't hold it against me. I was going to protect you," Tyler said.

"Tyler needs your support, Kels," Zach said.

Tyler glared at him. "I can handle Chris," he replied.

"Of course you can," Zach said doubtfully.

"He's not Lisa," Tyler commented.

"That's certainly true," Ryan said. "Kelsey should go, though. She won't let Chris talk you into something dumb."

"Like what?" Tyler asked him.

"Like testifying against Lisa," Ryan replied.

"I'm not going to," Tyler said. "This is between them."

"Chris is an idiot," Ryan said.

Tyler laughed. "You just don't like him."

"He's being mean to Lisa."

"Like Lisa's never been mean to him," Tyler said sarcastically.

Tyler and Kelsey were having lunch after Professor Surathi's class.

"He's amazing," Kelsey commented, breaking her soft sesame roll.

"I know," Tyler agreed, eating a spoonful of soup. "I can't believe how little I knew about copyright law," he continued after swallowing.

"I'll know everything I need to about copyrights for next summer after this, that's for sure," Kelsey commented.

"Do you want to focus on copyright?" Tyler asked her.

"Maybe. Alex Carsten suggested that I do patents," Tyler looked at her in interest.

"Patents?" Tyler asked. "Oh, because you're a biology major."

Kelsey nodded. "But I'd probably have to go back to school for a Ph.D. if I wanted to work on biology patents. A B.A. isn't enough."

"Do you want to do that?" Tyler asked.

"We'll see," Kelsey said. "I would make a lot of money as a patent lawyer."

"True," Tyler said. "Money isn't everything, though."

"Yeah, of course you'd say that," Kelsey teased.

Tyler laughed. "Chris says that I'm much too indifferent about money too." He sighed. "I think I can get through one dinner with him, but this is going to be a weird Christmas break."

"What do you mean? Are you going back to New York for Christmas?" Kelsey asked in surprise. She had assumed that Tyler wouldn't go back to New York to visit his father any time soon.

"I told Chris' girlfriend, Liz, that I would. I'm starting to regret that though. I don't know if I can handle two weeks there."

"Why spend the entire vacation with Chris?"

"I guess I could spend it in Medina and listen to Ryan moan about missing Jess," Tyler commented.

"Come home with me," Kelsey said.

"I couldn't impose on you," Tyler replied.

"Are you kidding? I'd love to have you visit me," Kelsey said. "It would be fun."

"Seriously?"

"Sure. You can meet my friends, and we can hang out. It's not like I've got big plans in Port Townsend, Washington," Kelsey said.

"What about your parents?" Tyler asked.

"They like when I bring friends home. Free help for the store," Kelsey teased.

Tyler laughed. "Well, I'd love to join you," he said.

"Great. Tell Chris you can't make it," Kelsey said.

"No, I'll have to go for at least part of the time. I promised Liz. But a week is probably enough," Tyler said. "Thanks, Kelsey."

"Don't thank me, you might be bored out of your mind," Kelsey commented.

"I can't imagine being bored with you," Tyler said.

"Today we're going to discuss the role of corporate boards," Professor Buxton said to the class. "And two of your classmates will have to forgive me, because Tactec is a perfect example of both the best and worst aspects of the corporate board."

Ryan and Tyler looked at each other.

"A corporate board is designed to represent the views of the shareholders to upper management in the running of a public company. In fact, the board members have a legal duty to the shareholders to do what is nominally in the shareholders' best interest. In reality though, it is the upper management that wields the power, because large corporate boards usually delegate decisions to the top executives, and accept their recommendations generally without fail.

"Tactec is a perfect example of this. The CEO of Tactec, Lisa Olsen, is well known for cultivating a board of yes-men. When upper management has the best interests of the shareholders in mind, this isn't necessarily a problem. However, sometimes the desires of the shareholders diverge significantly from those of the upper management, and when the board votes in lockstep with the top executives, they aren't representing the people that they are supposed to, the shareholders.

"Boards are supposed to bring their knowledge and business acumen to the corporation. But because directors are often less knowledgeable about the company than upper management, they often defer to the corporation's top executives. This is what largely happens at Tactec. As a high-tech company executive, Lisa Olsen has surrounded herself with board members from non-technology companies. This wouldn't be a problem if any of them had the guts to challenge her on anything, but she's seen to it that none of them do."

Erica raised her hand.

"Erica," Professor Buxton said.

"Why don't the shareholders just hire a new director for the board, if their views aren't being represented?"

"Well, that's a good question. Does anyone who isn't Tyler know the answer?" Professor Buxton said. Tyler smiled.

"It's too expensive," Zach said.

"Explain why," Professor Buxton said.

"When a shareholder wants to get rid of a board member, they have to communicate to all of the shareholders and convince a majority of them to vote against the board. In a large public corporation, there might be thousands of shareholders, and there's no guarantee that they will be knowledgeable enough to vote against the board. Usually shareholders give their proxy to the board so the board can vote their shares," Zachary said. "Anyone who wants to get rid of a board member better have a lot of money to lose."

"This is called a proxy fight, and in a company the size of Tactec it could cost between three to five million dollars," Professor Buxton explained. "The dissenting shareholder would need to contact every other shareholder and give them the option of choosing the alternate board member."

Professor Buxton continued, "In the meantime, the corporation is telling the shareholders how great everything is and will continue to be if the board remains the same. It's really an uphill battle for any dissenting shareholder. Usually the only people who are capable of launching a proxy fight are institutional investors, such as state pension funds or very rich shareholders with a lot of the company's stock."

"Has there ever been a proxy fight at Tactec?" Erica asked. Professor Buxton looked at Tyler, who answered.

"Twice. They both failed."

"Even if you manage to win the proxy fight, you're out the money for the battle, unless the board of directors decides to reimburse you," Professor Buxton added.

"So why would anyone begin a proxy fight?" Jessica asked.

"Because you have the quixotic belief you can win," Professor Buxton said. "It is possible to do so, but generally people only start proxy fights when they've exhausted every other avenue to get the board of directors to listen to their viewpoint."

"Professor Buxton, you said that Tactec represented the best and the worst of corporate boards. What's the best of Tactec?" Erica asked.

"Well, when management is making good decisions, having a board that doesn't get in the way of progress is a great thing. Lisa Olsen is a very capable CEO, so her missteps have been few and far between. However, Tactec's current obsession with acquiring Chen Industries might turn out to be one of those missteps and in this instance, a stronger board capable of telling the CEO no might be a good thing," Professor Buxton commented.

Kelsey saw Zach glance at Tyler. She remembered that Zachary had asked Tyler about the Taiwanese acquisition over the summer. Unlike Professor Buxton, Tyler had seemed to think the acquisition was a good idea.

"So who would you put on a board of directors, Professor?" Tyler asked.

"That's an interesting question. Do I want to keep my job as CEO and continue to do things my own way? Or am I actually interested in maintaining my duties to the shareholders?" Professor Buxton asked.

Tyler smiled. "Both."

"Well, if it were up to me, I would choose a board that was friendly to me as CEO, but wasn't afraid to get their hands dirty and find out a little bit about the company they were supposed to be running. A lot of companies will pick board members who have no idea what they are doing, and that way they can control them. Ultimately, though, I believe that's what leads to disaster. Without a board that is willing to rein in the excesses of the company, the company is likely to fail in the long term."

"But as a reigning CEO, are you really interested in the success of the company long-term? Or are you just concerned about keeping your job?" Jessica asked.

"As a CEO, you probably have a lot of stock in the company, so I imagine that both would be of some importance," Professor Buxton pointed out. "In the case of Tactec, since Lisa Olsen seems to have decided to pass the company on to the next generation, I suspect that her view of the importance of the long-term prospects of Tactec has changed."

Tyler leaned back in his seat.

"But if the company is doing well and delivering value for shareholders, what's the point of making changes in the board?" Zach asked.

"Perhaps there isn't a point, Mr. Payne, if you're looking at short- to mid-term gains. But consider the expectations of the shareholders. Do they want a company that will continue to grow, quarter after quarter, or one that becomes stagnant because the board didn't have the foresight to have a vision a decade or more into the future? Not everyone is a venture capitalist looking for the next thing. Many of Tactec's shareholders are hoping for stock in a company that they can pass on to their grandchildren."

"So did you learn anything for your upcoming reign as CEO?" Zach asked Tyler at lunch.

"Funny," Tyler said.

"What do you think of the board at Tactec?" Kelsey asked Tyler.

"Professor Buxton's right. They are a bunch of yes-men," Tyler commented. "And that's the way my mother likes it."

"He didn't think much of the Taiwan acquisition," Zach said.

"Because he doesn't know what we do about Chen Industries," Tyler replied.

"And what's that, Mr. Olsen?" Zach asked.

"By we, I meant me," Tyler said. "I told you, I'm not telling you anything."

Zach laughed. Ryan offered Jessica a bite of his cornbread, which she took.

"When was the proxy fight?" Ryan asked Tyler. "I don't remember."

"We were young," Tyler said. "I don't think we were in high school yet. There were two, one right after the other."

"Do you remember it?" Jessica asked him.

"Vaguely. I remember Lisa giving a press conference around that time, and practicing in front of a public relations person in our living room."

"Why did they start the proxy fight?" Kelsey asked

"I don't remember," Tyler said.

"Probably because Lisa fired a Chief Financial Officer," Ryan said.

"That job has more turnover than any other at Tactec. How many have there been?" Zach said.

"Thirteen," Tyler said.

"Geez. Don't bother to hang up a picture of your family in the office," Jessica said.

"Lisa always hates them. I don't know why," Tyler said.

"Maybe that's where she should put Ryan. Then there'd be less turnover. Lisa would never fire Ryan," Zach commented.

"That's like the worst job ever," Ryan said. "Looking at spreadsheets all day. No thanks."

Jessica looked at him. "What was working at Tactec Legal like?"

"Fun. You should join me," Ryan said, smiling at her.

"I'm considering it. I really don't want to interview," Jessica said.

"That would be great," Ryan said to her.

"You'll really get nothing done if Jess is there," Tyler commented.

"You could work for my father," Ryan said.

"Doing what?" Zach said.

"He wants a new assistant, but someone with legal experience."

"Your dad's a lawyer."

"Yeah, but he gets sick of reading memos. He wants someone else to do it and tell him what he needs to know," Ryan commented.

"I can't imagine working for your father," Jessica said.

"You haven't met him yet. You'd probably like it," Ryan said.

"Right," Jessica said doubtfully.

"Interview at Collins Nicol," Kelsey said.

"Maybe," Jessica said.

"I can't believe you're the only one of us that needs to interview," Zach said.

"I shouldn't have worked in New York last summer," Jessica said.

"I told you so," Ryan pouted. Jessica grinned at him and gave him a kiss on the cheek.

"I know," she sighed. "Then again, I guess I could go back."

"No!" Ryan said. "I can't take another summer without you."

"Sure you could," Jessica said.

"No way," Ryan said. "You can't leave again."

"We'll see."

Kelsey was excited for the first Law Journal meeting, but to her surprise when she arrived, she was one of almost fifteen Darrow second-year students. She had known that it wasn't as elite as Law Review, but she was surprised that five times as many students had been selected for Journal than for Law Review, which only had three second-years. Very quickly, she discovered that since there were so many students, and the Law Journal was only published once per year, that Law Journal would take up very little of her time. In fact, she was only expected to edit and cite-check one article before February. At least, she thought as she left the meeting, she could put it on her resume.

Ryan and Jessica decided to join the yoga club. Jessica had decided that she needed a stress reliever besides her usual eating, and of course, Ryan, who already practiced meditation, joined as well. The yoga studio was directly across from the Law Review offices, and one floor above the Law Journal office. After the Law Journal meeting, Kelsey walked up to the Law Review offices.

"Hey, Kels," Tyler said as she walked in.

"Hi, Tyler," she replied. "I figured you'd be here."

"I would say I'm always here, but it isn't true this year."

"Yeah, Christian doesn't seem as intense as Sophia."

"It's like day and night," Tyler said to her. "How was your Law Journal meeting?"

"Fine. I don't have a lot to do," Kelsey said.

"Lucky you," Tyler said.

"Law Review's way more prestigious," Kelsey commented.

"Sure, and I do ten times as much work," Tyler replied.

"Actually, I think you'll be doing about twenty times more. I only have one article to cite-check," Kelsey said, shaking her envelope at him.

"Really? I've been assigned the task of helping Professor Janssen with his article this issue."

"Janssen?" Kelsey asked.

"He's new. Teaches First Amendment. He's very intense."

"That's why he was assigned to you?" Kelsey asked.

"Of course. Christian figured if I could deal with Sophia and Bill Simon, I could handle Janssen," Tyler said.

"Poor you."

"He's not too bad," Tyler said. "Anyway, I've got less to do this year, so I'm not complaining."

"Will you be here for a while?"

"No, I was just about to leave. Are you heading back home?" Tyler asked.

"I was going to get a snack on the way."

"Great, I'll join you," Tyler said. "Just let me get my bag."

Kelsey stood by the door as Tyler walked over to a chair and retrieved his bag. Kelsey noticed it was the bag that Zach had got him for his birthday.

"Do you like your gift?" she asked as they walked out of the offices and toward the elevator.

"The bag?" Tyler asked. "I actually do. I was surprised that Zach picked out something so nice for me."

"He did a good job," Kelsey said.

"So you helped him buy it?" Tyler asked.

"No, he picked it out himself," Kelsey replied.

"Really?" Tyler said as they walked off of the elevator.

"I just told him to buy you something," Kelsey said as they walked through the lobby.

"I really like it. It's not something I would have bought for myself," Tyler said to her.

They left the student center and began walking through the quad.

"On or off campus?" Tyler asked her.

"I was going to get a muffin on Madison," Kelsey said. Ryan had introduced her to a delicious chocolate chip muffin last school year, and she had wanted one all summer.

"Tired of Ryan's scones?" Tyler asked as they headed toward the back gate.

"Not really. I'm just in the mood for a muffin," Kelsey said. "Actually, I really miss Ryan's breakfasts and dinners."

"Me too. It was nice having a chef again," Tyler said.

Kelsey giggled. "You could live at home. You'd have Margaret."

"The price is too high," Tyler replied. "Although, if I eat the doorstops that they call pancakes at the dining hall one more time, I might change my mind."

"They're awful," Kelsey agreed as they headed down Madison Street.

"Where's the muffin shop?" Tyler asked her.

"It's a little cafe across from the bookstore," Kelsey said. "I went last year."

"What kind of muffin?" Tyler asked.

"Chocolate chip," Kelsey replied.

"Sounds great."

"They were amazing," Kelsey said. "I've been wanting one all summer, but I wasn't going to come up all this way for one."

They walked down the street and reached the spot where the cafe had been. Kelsey looked around.

"Wait, where's the cafe?" she said. She looked across the street. The bookstore was there, but the cafe where she had had her muffin with Ryan was gone.

"You're sure it was here?" Tyler asked.

"Positive," Kelsey replied. There was a tiny bistro where the cafe had been. "Darn."

"Sorry, Kels," Tyler said.

"It's okay. I was just really looking forward to one," she said. "I'll get a bagel instead."

Later that night, after dinner, there was a knock on the door. Jessica got up to answer it. It was Tyler, and he was holding a large plastic box.

"Hi," he said.

"Hey, Tyler. Come on in," Jessica said.

Kelsey looked up. "Hi, Tyler," she said.

"Margaret sent something over for you," he said. He walked over and handed her the box. Kelsey opened it. A dozen chocolate chip muffins were inside.

"Tyler. Thank you," Kelsey said in surprise.

"You're welcome," he said.

"You didn't have to do this," Kelsey said. But she pulled out one of the muffins.

"It's my pleasure," Tyler replied.

"Share," Jessica said.

"Oh, sorry," Kelsey said, handing Jessica the box. Jessica grinned and took out a muffin of her own.

"I was kidding, but thanks," Jessica said. Kelsey wasn't paying attention. She had removed the wrapper from the giant muffin and was biting into it.

"Yum," Kelsey said. "This is so good." It was even better than the one she had eaten on Madison last year.

"Let me have a bite," Tyler said. Kelsey held the muffin out to him and he took a bite.

"Delicious," Tyler said.

"Take some back with you," Kelsey said.

"No thanks," Tyler said. "They're for you."

"Tyler, that was really sweet of you," Kelsey said. "Thank you."

"Margaret likes you. She was happy to make them. I'll see you later," he said.

"Bye. And thanks again," Kelsey said.

"Thanks, Tyler," Jessica said, mouth full of muffin.

"Bye," Tyler said, and he left.

"So why are we eating muffins?" Jessica asked Kelsey.

"I wanted one this afternoon, but the store had closed."

"So Tyler had his chef whip some up for you?" Jessica asked in amusement.

"Yes, he did," Kelsey said, shaking her head.

"I would say that it was unbelievable, but I'm still trying to get rid of the pounds from all of the cookies Ryan had delivered to us first semester," Jessica said, taking another bite of her muffin.

"That was really nice," Kelsey said.

"We're so spoiled," Jessica said.

"I know. I mean, in my world, when the store closes, that means you don't get a muffin. Unless you make it yourself," Kelsey said.

"That's not your world anymore, now that you know Tyler," Jessica pointed out.

Kelsey picked up the phone. It was a phone call she had been dreading.

She was calling Jasmine to invite her and Morgan to Darrow, which was the good part of the phone call. Student services had decided that the fall event would be a campus-wide Halloween party, and Kelsey really wanted her friends to join her. They hadn't come to Darrow last year, since Kelsey knew that she would be panicked during her first year of law school, so they had remained in Port Townsend.

The part of the phone call she was dreading was talking to Jasmine. October was coming up, and in Jasmine's family that meant only one thing.

Jasmine's great grandfather was a doctor who had brought his family to Washington State from the South during the African-American migration around World War Two. When he had, he had also brought his no-smoking, no-drinking, healthy lifestyle with him. The way that the Jefferson family lived was the reason that the Norths had asked them to take in Kelsey for a few months when she was a troubled teenager.

During the three months Kelsey lived with them, she had had the displeasure of living through what was termed 'fit month' by the family. Every March and October, Jasmine and her mother went through the house and tossed out every bit of junk food that had sneaked in over the past five months. Take-out menus were stored, the pantry was stocked with healthy snacks, and everyone in the house was required to set a fitness goal for themselves.

It was Jasmine's favorite family tradition. Although she had the body of a fitness model, Jasmine always set new goals and blew through them. During the fit month that Kelsey had been with the Jeffersons, attempting to avoid the rules was the one thing she and Jasmine's annoying older brother, Jace, agreed on. They had driven to the McDonald's in Sequim, forty-five minutes away, to avoid getting caught by a nosy neighbor, twice during the month,

Ever since, Jasmine always nagged Kelsey and Morgan to join in. And Kelsey usually felt guilty enough to do so. It was such part of Jasmine's life, that her fiance Jim had joined in last March, and he had lost ten pounds.

Freshman year of college, and last year, Kelsey had begged off, and Jasmine had let her get away with it. But there would be no getting out of it this year.

Actually, Kelsey had to admit, a fit month was just what she needed right now. Thanks to moving in with Ryan and Tyler, weeks of take-out and Ryan's excellent cooking, plus the chocolate chip muffins she had devoured recently, Kelsey's jeans had become quite a bit tighter. In fact, she had been forced to put two pairs aside, exchanging them for sweatpants. She knew she had gained at least five pounds, and because she had refused to step on a scale, it was very possible that she had gained more. If she had any hope of going to the Tactec holiday event without telling Jeffrey that she needed a bigger size, she needed to take part.

Kelsey dialed Jasmine, who picked up instantly.

"North! What's up?" Jasmine asked.

"Hey, Jazz," Kelsey said. "I want you and Morgan to come over for Halloween."

"Seriously? That would be amazing. We're there," Jasmine said. "Are you going to join me for fit month this year? Morgan and Jim are already on board."

Kelsey sighed to herself.

"Of course," she said unwillingly.

"Great!" Jasmine said. "Tell you what. Since you're doing fit month with us, I'll bring your costume."

Kelsey was silent.

"So, North. What do you think?" Jasmine asked her over the phone. Kelsey was sitting on the sofa, her Securities casebook to her side.

"I think I'm regretting that I invited you and Morgan to the Halloween party," Kelsey teased.

"Oh, come on. It will be fun. Don't you trust me to pick out your costume?" Jasmine said.

"No," Kelsey replied honestly.

"Morgan said it was okay," Jasmine pouted.

"Morgan's crazier than I am."

"Hardly. Look, everything important will be covered," Jasmine said.

"Oh, great," Kelsey said.

"Kelsey," Jasmine replied.

"Fine," Kelsey said, defeated. "I'll wear what you want me to."

"Cool!" Jasmine said. "So here's the deal. Josh says…"

"Josh who?"

"The fitness blogger," Jasmine said, impatiently.

"Right, of course," Kelsey said. He was the only Josh she and Jasmine knew in common.

"He said that you need to give yourself a goal to stay fit, and he said that Halloween was the perfect time for that. We have almost six weeks to get into perfect shape for our costumes. I thought it would be fun to do it together."

"But I can't know what I'm wearing?"

"No. Just get into the gym," Jasmine said.

Kelsey sighed silently. Kelsey was wondering what she was signing up for. Jasmine always picked out sexy clothes for Kelsey to wear, even though Jasmine's own style leaned closer to cute. Some days Kelsey felt she was Jasmine's live version of a Barbie doll, with the long blonde hair to match.

"Are you and Morgan wearing the same thing as I am?"

"A variation," Jasmine replied.

"But you won't be more covered up than I will?" Kelsey asked.

"No," Jasmine replied. "We'll be a matched set."

"Okay, Jazz. Just remember that I go to school here, so nothing too embarrassing."

"You'll look hot."

"That's what I'm afraid of," Kelsey replied.

On Friday evening, Tyler and Kelsey walked into a bistro in Pike Place Market. A man stood up and waved at them. To Kelsey's surprise, he looked nothing like Tyler. They walked over to him and he gave Tyler a big hug.

"Ty, it's great to see you," he said. "And this must be Kelsey."

"Hi, Mr. Davis," Kelsey said, holding out her hand. He moved it aside and gave her a gentle hug.

"Chris," he corrected her kindly. "Sit, you two. I just got here."

"How's the Inn at the Market?" Tyler asked him.

"Excellent. Great choice, Ty," Chris replied. He handed both of them menus. "So, how's your mother?"

"The same as always," Tyler replied.

"I was sort of surprised that I wasn't stopped at the city limits," Chris quipped.

Tyler laughed. "I'm stuck now," he said, looking at the menu. "Mom isn't worried anymore."

Chris looked at his son, a little sadly. "If anyone can outsmart Lisa Olsen, it's you," he said.

"I'm working on it," Tyler replied. "Kels, do you see what you want?"

"I'm trying to decide between the tortellini and the cioppino," she replied.

"How about you, Chris?"

"Fish and chips," Chris replied. "It's weird being back here. Seattle is so different now."

"When was the last time you were here, Chris?" Kelsey asked.

"Tyler was three. A long time," Chris said, putting the menu aside.

"Are you originally from Seattle?" Kelsey asked.

"Idaho," Chris replied. "Ty, what are you having?"

"Steak," Tyler said. He closed the menu. "How's Liz?"

"She's good. She just got back from a conference herself." Tyler nodded. "She wants you to come spend some real time with us this summer."

"I'd like to," Tyler said. "But I don't think I'm going to have time."

"Have you gotten an internship yet?" Chris asked.

"I'll be working for Simon and Associates again," Tyler replied.

"Not Taylor, Smart and Mayer?" Chris grinned.

"Absolutely not," Tyler replied. The waitress came over and took their orders.

"So what happened with the law firm Lisa destroyed?" Chris asked after she left.

"It's gone," Tyler said, shrugging. "I think a few of the lawyers have found jobs at Taylor, Smart and Mayer, but Tactec mostly wanted a clean slate."

"Did Tactec win the overbilling case?"

"Not yet. But they probably will. The law firm was overbilling like crazy," Tyler replied.

"How is your mother?"

"One guess," Tyler replied.

"She hasn't changed at all," Chris said. The waitress brought over their drinks. Chris took a sip of his. "On the other hand, you turned out well."

"In spite of?" Tyler quipped.

"I didn't say that," Chris grinned, taking another drink. "Remember, Tyler, I'm not allowed to 'defame, slander, or comment in any way disparagingly about Ms. Olsen.'"

Tyler laughed.

"Never marry a lawyer," Chris said. "No offense, kids."

"None taken," Tyler replied.

"Well, when you do get married, Ty, make sure you send me a copy of the prenup. You'll need a truck to carry it."

"You should see the pages of trust documents I've had to sign," Tyler replied.

"Lisa has gotten a lot of blowback for giving the money to you. Did you find out why she did it?"

"Ryan says it's because of you."

"Me?"

"She didn't want me to go back to New York and work."

"And now you can't because you're tied to Tactec. Nothing gets past her."

"That's why I can't work in New York next summer either. She's lined up a bunch of unnecessary board meetings that I 'must' attend."

"What does Bob's kid think about all of this?"

"Ryan's thrilled. He always wanted the money."

"Like father, like son," Chris said. He smiled at Kelsey. "I'm allowed to disparage Bob Perkins," he said. "What wife is Bob on now?"

"He just divorced number four," Tyler said.

"She get anything?"

"Not a dime. Mom's been writing the prenups since Bob divorced number two," Tyler said.

"Of course she has," Chris said thoughtfully. "So have you thought about what I said?"

"No," Tyler replied.

"Ty. I don't want to have to fight you too," Chris said.

"Then don't. Drop the lawsuit," Tyler said.

"Do you know what we're talking about?" Chris asked Kelsey.

"She knows," Tyler answered for Kelsey. "Kelsey's read the countersuit."

"Tyler, what Lisa did was wrong."

"Of course it was. But it's over," Tyler said, as the waitress brought over their appetizer. Kelsey took a sip of her drink. She knew that she was here to support Tyler, but it was strange to watch him argue with his father.

"It's not over," Chris said.

"Are you really going to subpoena me?" Tyler asked him. Chris sighed, and picked up one of the potatoes. He ate it.

"My lawyer will," Chris said, once he had finished chewing.

"Why? I have nothing to do with this."

"Tyler, you have everything to do with this," Chris countered.

"I've forgiven her. Why won't you?"

"You haven't forgiven her at all," Chris replied. "You can't stand her."

"That's not true," Tyler said.

"Really?" Chris said doubtfully.

"Really. I love my mother," Tyler said. "I just don't always agree with her methods."

"Why won't you help me?"

"This isn't helping you," Tyler said. "Anyway, I just want to live my life. I don't want to have my childhood spread all over the press. I won't have any privacy left if you do this."

"Tyler, I don't have a choice. I can't let Lisa get away with this."

"She's not getting away with anything. Anyway, it's just money. You won't get my school years back."

"Just money, Tyler Davis? Like it's nothing?"

"Chris, if I could, I'd write you the check myself," Tyler said.

"Tyler, your testimony is important. I can't win without it."

"Then you can't win," Tyler said. "I don't want to do this, and I'm going to do everything I can not to."

Chris frowned and ate another potato. Kelsey glanced at Tyler. She noticed that he wasn't eating. She speared one of the potatoes with her fork and offered it to him. Tyler glanced at her, smiled, but shook his head. Kelsey ate the potato on her fork.

"Tell Lisa's lawyers whatever you like. We're still going to subpoena you," Chris said.

"I have lawyers of my own," Tyler said. Chris looked him at surprise.

"You aren't represented by Lisa's goons?"

"No," Tyler said. "I need to protect myself against both of you."

Chris laughed. "I'm doing this for you."

"You're doing this for yourself," Tyler replied. "If you win, Lisa's just going to write you a check. Nothing else will change, except that you'll hate each other more."

"I don't understand how you can just live with this."

"I've been living with it for most of my life," Tyler replied. "Chris, don't do this."

"It's done," Chris said. "Fine, let's not discuss this all evening. I'm only here for the night. How's school?"

"Okay," Tyler said. He took a potato and ate it.

"How is Law Review this year?"

"Better," Tyler replied. "The editor's more pleasant."

"Good. You're still coming to New York for the holiday?"

"Part of Christmas. I'm supposed to have Thanksgiving with Lisa."

"Fourth quarter, right? Lisa will be working all of December?"

Tyler nodded.

"Your mother ruined two Christmases with that nonsense," Chris said.

Tyler sighed. He ate a potato, as did Kelsey. The waitress came over and took the plate away.

"Chris, I know that you're angry," Tyler said, once he had finished chewing, "But we need to move on."

Tyler's father frowned at him.

"Ty, you have no idea what it means to move on," Chris said. "You're just a child."

"No, I was a child. But now I'm an adult and I know that this isn't the right thing to do."

"Tyler, you didn't have to live with the knowledge that your son was across the country, locked behind a gate, because your spiteful ex-wife wanted to hurt you." Chris said. "I did. So you're wrong. This is exactly the right thing to do."

"So you're doing it. Fine. Do it without me," Tyler snapped. He glanced up as the waitress placed their plates in front of them.

"No," Chris said. "In her filing, Lisa claimed that you didn't want to see me. Is that true?"

Tyler looked at his father. "It doesn't matter what I wanted then. I don't want to be a part of this now."

"That isn't an answer," Chris said.

"Lisa's given me one hundred thousand dollars, just to fight you. Do you have any idea how much she's willing to spend for herself?" Tyler said, ignoring his father's question.

"It doesn't matter. I'm not going to let her win this time."

"Chris, you can't afford to stop her," Tyler said.

"Tyler, stop arguing with me," Chris ordered. Tyler sat back in his seat, clearly frustrated. But he said nothing more. He cut into his steak. Kelsey speared a tortellini and ate it.

The rest of the dinner was tense, but discussions about the lawsuit ended. They discussed the gallery, people in New York, and the classes that Tyler and Kelsey were taking this year. After Chris paid the bill for their meal, the three of them stood on the street to say their goodbyes, the neon red Public Market sign illuminating their backs.

"Think about what I said, Ty," Chris said, shaking Tyler's hand.

"I've made my decision, Chris," Tyler replied. Chris frowned.

"It was nice to finally meet you," Chris said to Kelsey. "Good luck with your school year."

"Thanks," Kelsey said.

Chris looked at Tyler for a final time, then jaywalked across the street, back to his hotel. Tyler and Kelsey walked up the hill to First Avenue. Once they reached it, Tyler spoke.

"Everyone knows what's best for me, even when they don't," he commented.

"True," Kelsey said. "You have to decide for yourself in the face of everyone else's opinion."

"Somedays I wish I had a neutral party. Someone who was only interested in what was right for me," Tyler said. Kelsey was silent. Although she could play that role in his dispute with Chris, there were other issues about Tyler's life that she definitely couldn't remain indifferent about.

Tyler looked at her.

"Thanks for coming. Chris couldn't yell at me as much in front of you."

"It was nice to meet him. He wasn't what I was expecting."

"No?"

"I guess I was surprised that he looks nothing like you."

"I take after my mother," Tyler commented. "Chris is about to find that out."

"What are you going to do?"

"Fight to keep my private life private. If Chris wants a battle, he's going to get one," Tyler replied.

Tyler and Kelsey walked into the boys' apartment on Monday after class. Zachary was sitting on the sofa, bare-chested with pajama pants on. An envelope was sitting on the coffee table in front of him.

"Didn't make it to class today?" Tyler asked, putting his bag next to the sofa.

"Yeah. Sorry," Zach said.

"Sorry?" Tyler asked. Zach handed him the envelope and Tyler opened it.

"Chris served you," Zach explained.

Tyler sighed.

"I wondered how they'd find me. Thanks, Mr. Payne," Tyler said, opening the envelope.

"I know. I'm sorry," Zach said.

"They don't have to serve you personally?" Kelsey asked.

"Just someone at the house," Tyler said. "Next time I'm dragging you out of bed."

"You can't avoid him forever," Zach said.

"I could have avoided him for a few more days," Tyler said, scanning the document. "They want to depose me next month. I'd better give this to Simon."

"Simon?" Zach asked.

"He's going to help me write the motion to quash," Tyler replied. "Princess, do you want to come downtown with me? I'll buy lunch."

"Princess?" Zach said in interest.

"You were dreaming, Zach," Kelsey said sharply.

"Right," Zach said. "That must be it."

"I'll go," Kelsey said. "Then Zach can go back to sleep."

"Don't answer the door again," Tyler said to him. "Let's go, Kels," he said. Tyler and Kelsey left the apartment, took the elevator outside, and went out to the parking lot. Tyler opened the door for Kelsey and they got in. Tyler tossed the envelope on the back seat, they put on their seat belts, and Tyler drove out of the lot.

Kelsey looked at Tyler's handsome, serious face.

"What are you thinking?" she asked.

Tyler sighed. "I'm thinking that Chris is going to be really angry with me."

"You could agree to the deposition," Kelsey said.

"No. That isn't an option," Tyler said as they drove down Madison Street. "I'll just have to deal with Chris later."

"He's your father. I'm sure things will improve," Kelsey said positively.

Tyler glanced at her and smiled. "Has your father ever subpoenaed you?"

"No."

"I'm not sure that Chris and I have a normal father-son relationship," Tyler commented.

"You have a lifetime to work things out," Kelsey said.

"If we don't sue each other to death first," Tyler replied.

Tyler drove them to Simon and Associates and they went up to the offices. They said hello to the receptionist and Tyler led Kelsey to Bill Simon's office.

"He just sent it over?" Bill Simon said in lieu of a greeting.

"This morning," Tyler said, handing him the envelope.

Simon opened it and looked it over. "Were you served properly?"

"Yes, unfortunately," Tyler replied.

"He's not asking for documents?" Simon asked Tyler.

"No. What would he ask for?" Tyler replied.

Simon said nothing and kept reading. He finally looked up.

"What do you want to do?"

"Avoid being deposed," Tyler said.

"Completely?"

"I want a protective order. I want nothing to do with this case."

Simon smiled at him. "The case is about you," he commented.

"It's about money. Not me," Tyler replied.

"Fine. Do you know where to start?"

"Not really."

"Let's see. They want to do it here in Seattle, on a Saturday two weeks from today. They mention that they'll pay you for your mileage and time. When was the case filed?"

"This summer."

"Which means that they're still in discovery. There are no procedural problems to object to. What do you want to argue? That your testimony is irrelevant?"

"I'd like to," Tyler said.

"That's going to be a difficult one, Tyler," Simon said. "They're arguing over your childhood."

"It's that, or I can argue that the testimony covers privileged communications. But I don't know what Chris is going to ask me, so I'm not sure how to argue privilege," Tyler said.

"He hasn't given you a clue?"

"Nothing."

"All right. Start with an argument about relevance. I'm not sure you'll win though. Send it to me by Wednesday."

"Okay," Tyler said.

"Okay? You aren't going to ask me for more time? You must not be very busy at Darrow this year. Or perhaps you're going have Miss North to do your work for you again?" Simon winked at Kelsey, who stifled a giggle.

"Wednesday is fine," Tyler said testily.

"Check with your mother's office. See if they have any idea what he's going to ask about. I'd really like to be able to make a privilege argument."

"I will," Tyler replied. "Can I make an undue burden argument?"

"You're a student, and they want a Saturday morning. What do you think?"

"Maybe not," Tyler said in disappointment.

"That would be correct," Simon said.

"I haven't been doing this for twenty years," Tyler commented.

"With questions like that, I'm wondering if you've been doing this for twenty minutes," Simon retorted.

"Thanks for your support," Tyler replied with sarcasm.

"I'm not here to support you. I'm here to help you win," Simon said, handing the subpoena back to Tyler.

"Fair enough. Thank you," Tyler conceded.

"Wednesday," Simon said, returning to his computer. "Nice to see you, Miss North."

"Bye, Mr. Simon," Kelsey said. She and Tyler left the office.

"What do you want to eat?" Tyler asked as they walked out of the offices and headed to the elevator.

"Anything," Kelsey said. "Do you need help with research?"

Tyler shook his head. "No, thanks. I have a feeling I'm not going to get out of this." They got on the elevator and headed toward the parking lot.

"Simon didn't seem very optimistic," Kelsey agreed.

"What a nightmare," Tyler said as they reached the car. He let them inside.

As they drove out of the building, Tyler dialed his phone and put it on hands-free.

"Hi, Tyler."

"Hi, Mom," Tyler said. "Chris served me this morning. I just left Simon's office."

"Did he ask for documents?" Lisa asked him.

"Nothing. Has he told your lawyers anything about what he's going to ask me?"

"Not a word. When does he want the dep?"

"Next month."

"You wanted to get to know him. Now you do," Lisa commented.

"You married him," Tyler replied.

Lisa laughed. "Very true, Tyler Davis. That I did. But I got you out of it."

"You had me, anyway," Tyler replied. "I was practically at the wedding."

"You certainly kicked your way through it," Lisa replied.

"So you don't know what he wants," Tyler said.

"Except for the thirty million dollars, no," Lisa replied. "Didn't you see him last weekend?"

"I did, but he didn't tell me anything," Tyler said.

"No surprise there."

"Okay, thanks Mom."

"Let me know if you need more money. I have plenty put aside for this,"

Lisa said brightly.

"I will. Thanks."

"Love you," Lisa said.

"I love you too, Mom," Tyler said. He disconnected.

"Kelsey, are burgers okay?" Tyler asked her.

"As long as you aren't driving me back to the Darrow dining hall, I'm fine," Kelsey replied.

"Is it just me, or did the food get worse this year?" Tyler said.

"I don't think it's just you. I thought maybe it was because I ate so much of Ryan's great cooking this summer."

"Maybe that's it," Tyler said. "We need to convince him to cook every day. For five. No more of this just cooking dinner for Jessica."

Kelsey giggled. "I agree. Can I buy lunch for you today?"

"Absolutely not," Tyler said, turning into a parking lot.

"Tyler, you and Ryan paid for everything this summer."

"So?" Tyler said parking the car.

"It's not fair to you," Kelsey said. Tyler looked at Kelsey.

"You're kidding, right?" he said.

"No," Kelsey said. "It bothers me."

"Don't let it," Tyler said, getting out of the car.

"Why not?"

"Because I like to pay for you," Tyler said as they walked to the restaurant.

"Why?" Kelsey asked.

"Because I can't give you my time. All I can give you is my mother's money," Tyler replied.

"You're giving me your time now," Kelsey said. They entered the restaurant and were seated.

"I'm eating lunch with you. That isn't giving you my time," Tyler said.

"Of course it is."

"Someday, I hope in the not-too-distant future, I would like to spend time with you, where for once, we can talk about you and your dreams. That day you can buy me lunch," Tyler said.

"Tyler, no relationship is like that. There's always struggles and issues, and sometimes one person needs more support than the other," Kelsey said.

"You have never needed my support. I always seem to need yours," Tyler replied.

"I needed your support when Dylan left. And you gave it to me," Kelsey corrected him.

Tyler silently looked at the menu. Kelsey glanced at him and smiled to herself. For once, Tyler Olsen had been wrong.

After she had had lunch with Tyler and returned to her apartment, Kelsey looked at her phone. There was a new message from Alex Carsten.

Hi, Miss North.

Hi, Alex, Kelsey replied

It's time for dinner. When do you want to go? Saturday?

Saturday would be fine, Kelsey wrote. Alex had invited her out to dinner before she had left Collins Nicol, and now that she was settled back into Darrow, it seemed like a good time.

Good. I'm looking forward to it. Send me your new address and I'll pick you up.

Kelsey typed her address into the phone.

Thanks, 7 p.m.? Alex typed.

7 is fine. See you then.

See you Saturday, Miss North.

Kelsey was running on the treadmill the next morning as Jeffrey and a very fit woman wearing black workout clothes walked into the apartment gym.

"Good morning, Jeffrey," Kelsey called out pleasantly.

"Good morning, Miss North. Have you seen Tyler this morning?" Jeffrey replied.

"Not yet. He's a little late," Kelsey replied. Usually Tyler was in the gym by the third song on her mp3 player, but she was almost done with her run.

Out of the corner of her eye, she could see Jeffrey looking for something in his briefcase. He frowned.

"I'm sorry, Miss North, but can I ask a favor of you?" Jeffrey said to Kelsey.

Kelsey slowed her run to a walk and took out her earbuds. "Of course," she replied.

"This is Patricia. She's going to be coaching Tyler on how to use the new kettlebells. I'm concerned that Tyler has forgotten that he has an appointment with her, and of course, today I've left the keys to the apartment on my desk. Would you mind making sure he's up and on his way?"

"Sure," Kelsey said. She turned and got off of the treadmill. "I'll be right back."

Kelsey took the stairs up and walked to the boys' apartment. Zach had made it clear that if either she or Jess wanted to come into the apartment before noon, they were to use their keys, not the bell, to do so. Kelsey opened the boys' door quietly and walked to Tyler's bedroom. She knocked on the door. She could hear Tyler get up and walk over to the door.

The door opened and Tyler stood in front of her rubbing his eyes tiredly. Kelsey was once again surprised at how unbelievably sexy Tyler was when he first woke up. She was so used to seeing him in his usual composed perfection, that when she saw him disheveled and vulnerable, it always threw her off her guard.

"Hi, Kelsey," he said yawning. His brown hair was tousled in a way that Kelsey wanted to reach out and rumple it some more.

Kelsey took a deep breath to calm herself. It was taking a lot of self-control not to push him back into the bedroom and close the door behind herself. "Your personal trainer is downstairs. Jeffrey asked me to come up," she finally said.

"Oh, right. Thanks. Can you please let them know I'll be right down?" he said sleepily.

"Sure," Kelsey said. She bit her lip and turned away from him. Then she practically ran out of the apartment door.

She was flushed when she returned to the gym. She hoped that Jeffrey would assume it was from her workout. It wasn't.

Patricia was flipping through a folder, and Jeffrey was checking messages when she walked in. "Tyler will be down in a minute," Kelsey said to them after she composed herself.

"Thank you, Miss North," Jeffrey said, looking up at her. Kelsey nodded and got back on the treadmill.

She finished her run and was just getting off the treadmill as Tyler walked in, wearing his workout clothes. Kelsey glanced at him. Back to the normal level of sexy she was used to.

"Kels, do you want to join us?" Tyler asked her.

"Okay," Kelsey said, walking over. If she was going to have to do fit month, she might as well learn something new.

"Tyler," he said to the trainer, as he shook hands with her.

"Patricia," she replied.

"I'm Kelsey," Kelsey said, shaking Patricia's hand.

"Hi," Patricia said.

"Tyler, I'm heading to your mother's office. Let me know if you need anything," Jeffrey said.

"Okay, thanks," Tyler replied.

"Thank you for your help, Miss North," Jeffrey said.

"No problem, Jeffrey. Bye," Kelsey replied. Jeffrey left the room.

Patricia looked at Tyler and Kelsey. "So what's your goal?" she asked politely.

"I just wanted to learn how to use the kettlebells without hurting myself," Tyler said, laughing. "What about you, Kels?"

"I'm supposed to be doing a fitness challenge in October, so I guess anything that could help me with that would be great."

"A fitness challenge?" Tyler asked.

"It's my friend's idea. You eat super healthy and exercise consistently for a full month."

"What are you trying to achieve at the end of the month?" Patricia asked.

"A better body," Kelsey said.

"What does that mean to you?" Patricia asked.

Kelsey thought for a moment. "I'd like to have more muscular arms and a flatter stomach," she concluded.

"Kettlebells can help with that," Patricia said. She made a note in the book she had. "I can demonstrate a few exercises that you can try."

"That would be great," Kelsey said. "Thanks."

"No problem."

Tyler looked at Kelsey. "You aren't fit enough, Miss North?" he asked in amusement.

"Perfection is always just right out of our grasp, Mr. Olsen," Kelsey retorted.

Tyler laughed.

Patricia spent the next forty-five minutes demonstrating the proper use of the new kettlebell set. She helped both Kelsey and Tyler determine which was the proper weight for each of them to use, and gave Kelsey a number of exercises that she could use to tone her arms and belly. One of the exercises required Tyler's participation: Kelsey did a sit-up, kettlebell in hand, and passed it to Tyler, who grabbed it, lay down, did a sit-up and returned it to her.

"I'm going to die," Tyler groaned, lying on his back when it was Kelsey's turn to hold the kettlebell.

"Embrace the suck, Tyler," Kelsey said, passing the kettlebell back to him.

Tyler did his set, then lay back down again.

"I'm thinking you missed your calling by coming to Darrow. However, you're still young enough to join the Marines," he commented.

"If I did that, who would whip you into shape?" Kelsey asked. "Get up," she added.

Tyler groaned, and took the kettlebell. "This may have been the worst purchase of my life," he said, doing his sit-up. He passed it back to her.

"It's awesome," Kelsey said, doing her sit-up.

"Says you," Tyler replied. "I'm done."

"No way!" Kelsey replied. "It's your turn." Kelsey passed the kettlebell to him. Tyler took it and did his sit-up.

"That's good for now," Patricia said, taking the kettlebell from Tyler.

"Really?" Kelsey said.

"Thank you," Tyler said, slowly rising.

"She only stopped us because you're paying her," Kelsey whispered as Patricia's back was turned.

"I'll be paying her double as a bonus," Tyler retorted.

As Patricia was leaving to go, Tyler spoke.

"So, Kelsey when does your fit month start?" he asked.

Kelsey frowned. "Now," she said, thinking of her jeans.

"Patricia, why don't you plan to come through October twice a week to train Kelsey. Tuesdays and Thursdays, same time, okay?"

"Sounds good," Patricia said.

"Train Kelsey? What about you?" Kelsey asked Tyler.

"Me?"

"I'm not doing this without you," Kelsey said.

"I'll do my usual workout around the same time."

"Nope," Kelsey said.

Tyler sighed. "Fine. I'll join you."

Kelsey smiled at him.

"But you have to wake me up in the morning," Tyler continued.

Oh, boy. Kelsey thought.

At lunch, Kelsey and Ryan were reading an article on Ryan's iPad.

"I won't work with Dara Smith": Kim Chan's take on the controversy

Supermodel Kimberly Chan has decided that she wants the final word in the Dara Smith / Ryan Perkins showdown. The well known Chan, who was famously discovered by Ryan Perkins, and has gone on to advise many young models on her own, had this to say last night at the L.A. premiere of the new movie "Day and Night.'

"Ryan could have taken me or any of a thousand women to his event, but he asked Dara because he knew what the publicity could mean to a brand new girl. And to take advantage of such generosity, well, that's outrageous.

"Ryan's such a sweetheart that he didn't even say anything until Dara said that they were engaged.

"I just think that when you have people who support the modeling community the way that Ryan Perkins has over the years, that it's important for people to take a stand.

"That's why I've told my agency that I won't work with Dara Smith, and I've asked my friends to consider not working with her either. Every new model has been there, felt that desperation to be discovered, but it's not right to use people the way that Dara Smith did. "

According to several insiders, Kim Chan's crusade has already had an impact.

"I think that a lot of people in the fashion world are dismayed at what Dara Smith has done. Of course to make it in fashion, you need publicity, but Dara completely did it the wrong way. Because she got greedy, she's destroyed the opportunity for lots of other girls who will follow behind her. If I were Ryan, I would never take a brand new model to an event again." said one agency booker.

"Already I've heard that there have been quite a few cancelled bookings for Dara, and at least one cosmetic company that was considering her as new face for the brand, has backed away. Personally, if I was her agency, I'd drop her. Dara Smith has become too much of a liability."

Another insider had this to say, "Now that Kimberly Chan has spoken out, Dara Smith is going have trouble finding people on her side. Kim is well known for mentoring new models, and she has said that she feels a real responsibility to Ryan since she suggested he meet Dara in the first place. I think that Dara's fifteen minutes of fame are almost up."

In the meantime, Dara Smith has been surprisingly quiet. After Ryan Perkins' post disavowing a relationship with her, Dara has made no more posts on any of her social media accounts."

"I feel sorry for Dara," Ryan said. Tyler glanced at him.

"She broke up your relationship and you feel sorry for her?" Tyler asked.

"She didn't mean to," Ryan said. "Dara didn't know about Jess."

"You are really too kind," Tyler commented.

"She made a mistake," Ryan said.

"I suppose," Tyler said doubtfully. "What are you going to do about it?"

"Do you think Jess would get mad if I reached out to Dara?" Ryan asked Kelsey.

Kelsey looked at Ryan. "Yep," she replied.

"I won't do anything, then," Ryan said. "Jess means too much to me."

"So, Kels. What are you giving Tyler for Christmas?" Jessica asked the next evening.

"I have no idea. It took me forever to think of something for his birthday."

"Yeah, I was thinking that about Ryan. But I had an idea."

"What is it?" Kelsey asked. Anything had to be better than the nothing she'd thought of so far.

"Want to learn how to knit?" Jessica asked.

"Knit?" Kelsey asked her.

Jessica nodded. "It isn't hard. I'll teach you. Then we can make something for the boys."

"Like a sweater?" Kelsey asked.

"No, that's too hard. I was thinking hats and scarves. That would be pretty easy," Jessica replied.

"Easy?" Kelsey said doubtfully.

"Very easy," Jessica said. "I made a scarf for my dad, and I've knit dozens of baby hats. It really isn't difficult."

"We'll have time?"

"Sure. We can just work on them in the evenings," Jessica said. "Come on, it will be fun."

"You're sure I can do it?" Kelsey asked.

"Of course," Jessica said. Kelsey looked at her, and Jessica nodded positively.

"Okay. What do we do?"

"I was thinking we'd go off campus and buy the yarn this weekend. Then I can teach you the basics on Sunday."

"Sounds good," Kelsey said.

"Think about what color Tyler wants. We can go after lunch on Saturday," Jessica said.

Saturday afternoon, Kelsey and Jessica rode the bus down Madison to a knitting store near the Arboretum. They walked into the store, which was lined with yarn on the walls. Kelsey marveled at all of the colors and textures.

"Have you thought of what color Tyler would like?" Jessica asked her as they walked in.

"Navy, of course."

Jessica laughed. "Of course. What could be more conservative?"

"What color are you getting for Ryan?"

"Green."

"Blue would bring out his eyes," Kelsey commented.

"I know, but he likes green," Jessica shrugged. She walked over to a large shelf with yarn.

"Do you ladies need any help?" a clerk asked them.

"Can you point us to some worsted weight wool?" Jessica asked her. "Something good for a scarf and hat."

"Right over here," the clerk said. She directed them to a large selection.

"What do you like, Kels?" Jessica asked her.

Kelsey looked at the wide array of choices. "Can we use any of these?" Kelsey asked.

"Sure," Jessica said, picking up a skein.

"Really?" Kelsey asked.

"They're all around the same thickness. Just pick one you think he'll like and I'll help you," Jessica said soothingly.

Kelsey found one that she liked, and looked at the price. "Wow."

"What?" Jessica asked.

"The price," Kelsey said.

Jessica wrinkled her nose. "I know. It's crazy."

"How many of these will we need?" Kelsey asked.

"It depends on the kind you buy. But probably a minimum of six," Jessica said.

"Okay. That's not too terrible," Kelsey replied. She replaced the skein of yarn and picked up a different one. "What do you think about this one?"

"Beautiful," Jessica said. She took it from Kelsey and looked at the label. "Navy Heather. 100% wool. It's very soft," she said, handing it back to her.

"I think I'll get this one," Kelsey said, touching it gently. "Do you see one you like?"

"I was deciding between these two," Jessica said, holding up two green skeins. One was a dark forest green, the other a lighter, brighter leaf green.

"I prefer the darker one," Kelsey commented.

"Me too. But I bet Ryan would like the lighter one better," Jessica said thoughtfully.

"Ryan will like whichever one you like," Kelsey said wisely.

Jessica laughed. "Yeah, you're probably right about that. Wait, how about this one?" she said, putting the two skeins of yarn she was holding aside, and picking up a soft fern green.

"That's really nice," Kelsey said.

"I'll get this one," Jessica said, looking at the label. "Let me see yours again," she said, holding out her hand. She took Kelsey's yarn and hers and took both to the counter. Jessica spoke to the clerk for a moment, as Kelsey looked at some of the other yarns on offer. Then Jessica returned.

"You'll need eight skeins and I'll need ten," Jessica said.

"Okay."

"Sorry. I should have warned you about the cost," Jessica said.

"It's fine," Kelsey said. "It's like one dinner with Tyler. Actually, it's probably cheaper."

Jessica laughed. Both girls got the required skeins of yarn, and took them to the front counter. Jessica pulled a pair of bamboo knitting needles from a display and a set of metal circular needles.

"You'll need these too," Jessica said. Kelsey nodded. They paid for their respective yarns.

"Do you need these wound?" the clerk asked.

"What?" Kelsey asked.

Jessica shook her head. "We'll do it at home, thanks." Each girl took her bag, and they left the store and headed to the bus stop.

"Do I need a pattern?" Kelsey asked.

"Not for this. It's easy," Jessica replied.

"What did the clerk mean about winding the yarn?"

"You wind it into a ball so you can knit with it easier," Jessica said. "They have a machine that does it, but we can just do it at home."

"Okay," Kelsey said, looking into her bag. She was pretty excited. She had never really done crafts before, except at school.

"We'll have fun. We have to hide it from the boys, though," Jessica said as the bus pulled up.

"Nice place," Alex said on Saturday night, looking around as Kelsey put on her fleece jacket. Jessica was out with Ryan.

"Thanks."

"No really, I lived in a dump in law school," Alex replied.

"Where did you go?"

"UVa," Alex said. "Ready?"

"I am," Kelsey replied.

She and Alex walked out of the apartment, and she closed the door behind them. To her surprise, Tyler was in the hall.

"Tyler Olsen," Alex said, extending his hand to Tyler.

"Mr. Carsten," Tyler replied, shaking it.

"How was your summer?"

"Great," Tyler replied. He glanced at Kelsey, then back at Alex.

"Going back for seconds with Bill Simon? I haven't seen your resume cross my desk yet."

"I'll be back at Simon and Associates next summer," Tyler replied.

"A glutton for punishment. Well, good luck," Alex commented.

"Thank you," Tyler replied.

"Let's go, Kelsey," Alex said to her. He began to walk down the hall.

"Bye, Tyler," Kelsey said, following him. Tyler nodded at her, turned away, and opened the door of his apartment. Kelsey heard the door close firmly, as the elevator doors opened and she and Alex got in.

A half an hour later, she and Alex were in a pub on Capitol Hill. They had ordered and were sipping their drinks.

"What do you think of Professor Surathi? Rumor has it that he's an IP genius," Alex asked her.

"He's really smart," Kelsey agreed. "I've learned a lot about copyrights already this semester."

"How are your other classes?"

"Great. I like all of my professors this year," Kelsey said, stirring her Coke with a straw. A bright yellow lemon slice floated on top.

"Darrow is well known for having the best ones in the country. So you'll be ready for Collins Nicol next summer?"

"I think so," Kelsey said confidently.

"How well do you know Tyler Olsen?" Alex asked her.

"Pretty well," Kelsey admitted.

"Why is he working for Bill Simon again? I know Mary White put a full court press on him at the summer party to come to Collins Nicol next year."

"Tyler thought he learned a lot with Bill Simon," Kelsey said diplomatically.

"He's an interesting kid," Alex mused. "If I had two billion dollars, I sure wouldn't be working for Bill Simon."

"No?"

"No way. I'd be on an island somewhere," Alex said, taking a drink.

"Tyler isn't that kind of guy."

"He seems very serious," Alex commented.

"He is," Kelsey said.

"I guess it must not be easy being Lisa Olsen's son."

"I don't think it is," Kelsey agreed.

"What is your family like?"

"Normal," Kelsey replied. "My parents run a sporting goods store in Port Townsend."

"Port Townsend's nice," Alex said. "That's where you're from?"

"I am. Have you been to Port Townsend a lot?"

"Not really. I've taken a couple of dates there," Alex said. "I guess that wouldn't work so well to impress you."

"No," Kelsey agreed.

"Most girls think it's quaint," Alex commented. "So where does Miss Kelsey North like to go on dates?"

Kelsey looked at Alex. She wasn't particularly comfortable with this line of questioning, despite the fact that she was sitting in a restaurant having a meal with him.

"Lots of places," Kelsey replied.

Alex leaned back in his chair. "Why do I have the distinct impression that this isn't going well?"

"I'm sorry," Kelsey said, honestly. "I guess having spent the entire summer trying to impress you with my work, it seems strange to be having a casual conversation with you."

Alex smiled at Kelsey.

"You did impress me. You're going to make a good lawyer," Alex said. "But I asked you out so we could get to know each other as friends."

"I know. It just seems weird," Kelsey said. The waitress brought over their meals. Alex took a fry off of his plate and ate it.

"Don't think so much, Miss North," he said.

"I don't know how not to," Kelsey admitted.

"You Darrow students are so intense," Alex commented. Kelsey giggled. "No, really, it's true. The Darrow guy who worked for Jamie this summer, I thought he was going to break something thinking so much." Alex took a bite of his burger.

"It's not like UVa is easy," Kelsey commented.

"No, but we do know how to relax," Alex said.

"I'll try," Kelsey said, eating a fry of her own.

"Good," Alex said. "Are you going back to Port Townsend for the holidays?"

"I am," Kelsey said. She took a bite of her burger. It was delicious.

"Don't you get bored there? It's great, but I don't know if I can imagine living there."

"I like it. Seattle's nice too, though. Where are you from originally?"

"Philadelphia."

"Do you go back for the holidays?" Kelsey asked him.

"I do. There's nothing I like better than a six-hour flight with a million other people trying to get back home," Alex said.

Kelsey laughed.

Alex grinned at her. "So do you want to stay in Seattle when you graduate?"

"I think so," Kelsey said.

"We haven't scared you off from intellectual property work yet?"

"Not yet. David Lim tried though," Kelsey said.

"Have you been avoiding people who need free legal advice like I recommended?" Alex asked her, taking another bite of his burger.

"Absolutely. If I learned nothing else, I learned that this summer," Kelsey replied.

"Good. Then I did my job," Alex said. "So what do you do besides study?"

"Not much," Kelsey admitted. "I like to run."

"You're an athlete?"

"No. I like to run," Kelsey said.

"Did you run track in school?" Alex asked her.

"Briefly," Kelsey replied.

"I played football," Alex said, eating a fry.

"Really?" Kelsey asked.

"I wasn't particularly good at it. But we won a state championship in high school," Alex said to her.

"Impressive," Kelsey said.

"What else do you like to do? What did you do this summer after work?"

Kelsey thought for a moment, and a smile crossed her face.

"I hung out with my friends," she replied.

"Yeah, first year as an intern isn't too taxing. Unless you're working for Bill Simon that is," Alex commented.

"What do you have against Bill Simon?"

"I guess I just don't understand why anyone would turn down Collins Nicol to work for him," Alex said, eating a fry.

"Tyler has his reasons," Kelsey commented.

"Does he, Miss North?"

"As you said, it isn't easy being Lisa Olsen's son. Why does Collins Nicol want him so badly?" Kelsey asked.

"I'm sure you know. Tyler Olsen is worth thousands in billables to whoever he works for, but it's wasted on Bill Simon, who won't take work from Tactec."

"Which is why Tyler works for him," Kelsey said.

Alex thought about that for a moment. "He really is a strange kid," he concluded.

"He just wants to be judged on his own merits," Kelsey said.

Alex shook his head. "Never going to happen. He's always going to be Lisa Olsen's son. There's no escaping that. I mean, unless he moves to Antarctica."

"I suppose that's true."

"How is it that you live down the hall from him?" Alex asked.

"His roommate is dating mine," Kelsey replied.

"Sweet. Young love in law school," Alex said with sarcasm.

"What's wrong with that?"

"Nothing I guess. I just can't imagine dating someone that I'm competing against."

Kelsey looked at him. "What about dating your co-worker?"

"That's different. I'm your superior. I wouldn't be competing against you."

"Collins Nicol lets people in the same department date?" Kelsey asked.

"Collins Nicol lets you do anything that you sign paperwork promising not to sue them for," Alex replied. "Of course, you aren't working for Collins Nicol now," he said. "What kind of guys do you usually date?"

Kelsey thought about the question. The last two people she had been on dates with were Lucas and Ryan. She wasn't sure what to make of that.

"I'm not sure I have a type," Kelsey said.

"Smart?" Alex guessed.

Kelsey giggled. She wasn't sure either of her most recent dates fell into that category.

"Maybe," she replied.

"What's so funny?"

"I haven't been having much luck in the dating category lately. Your question made me realize that," Kelsey explained.

"I'm having trouble believing that," Alex said.

"It's true," Kelsey said.

"It's probably because you think too much," Alex commented, taking another bite of his burger.

"That's probably true," Kelsey conceded.

"You're young. You should just have fun," Alex said to her.

"I'm not good with fun," Kelsey said.

"Actually, you seem like you'd be a lot of fun," Alex teased.

"You'd be surprised," Kelsey said.

"Are you flirting with me?" Alex asked her.

"Absolutely not," Kelsey said. But she realized at that moment that she was.

Alex leaned on the table and looked at her. Kelsey watched him as his eyes surveyed her face.

"I think I need to watch out for you, Miss Kelsey. You aren't as innocent as you seem," Alex said.

"Innocent until proven guilty," Kelsey said, eating a fry.

On Sunday evening, Jessica and Kelsey sat in their living room, bags of yarn at their feet. Jessica had taught Kelsey how to wind her yarn, and had taught her the basics of knitting. Kelsey was struggling.

"This can't possibly be right," Kelsey sighed. She handed the tangle of yarn hanging from the metal needles to Jessica, who laughed.

"Don't worry, you'll get the hang of it," she said, putting her own knitting aside. Kelsey glumly noted that Jessica already had the beginnings of a hat on her own needles. Jessica carefully began undoing the yarn on Kelsey's needles.

"How long did it take you to learn?" Kelsey asked.

"You just have to practice, Miss Type A," Jessica teased.

"It shouldn't be so difficult."

"It isn't. You just learned an hour ago. You're doing fine."

"Maybe I should buy Tyler another book," Kelsey said.

"Don't be silly. You just missed a few stitches," Jessica handed Kelsey her needles back.

To Kelsey's surprise, everything looked okay again. "Thanks," she said.

"Miss North," Kelsey heard someone call behind her as she was walking to the library on Monday.

She stopped and turned around. It was Zach.

"Hi, Zach," Kelsey said.

"I thought I told you not to date your co-workers," Zach scolded.

Kelsey looked at him. "It wasn't a date," she replied. And as far as Kelsey was concerned it wasn't. Despite the few moments of flirting, the evening had been G-rated.

"I think you aren't clear on the concept of what a date is," Zach said.

"Actually, I'm pretty clear on what a date is. Some other people aren't," Kelsey replied.

Zach laughed. "I suppose you have a point."

"I thought I might," Kelsey replied.

"So how did you figure out it was Alex Carsten who was interested in you?"

"He told me."

"But you aren't interested in him?"

"I don't know. What will you tell Tyler?" Kelsey asked him.

"Give me a break, Kels," Zach said.

Kelsey shook her head, and her blond ponytail bobbed. "Nope. Let Tyler worry," she said.

"You're really mean," Zach said.

Kelsey looked at Zach. She laughed. "Look, I'm just following Ryan's advice."

"You're following Ryan's advice? You must be desperate," Zach said.

"Not really," Kelsey said. "I'm just living my life."

Zach pouted. "Tyler's really upset," he said.

"Please," Kelsey said dismissively.

"It's true. You're making him nervous. Alex Carsten is a star in the Seattle legal community."

"I know," Kelsey said.

"You know. You're doing this on purpose."

"Look, Zach, Alex asked me to dinner. I said yes. It's not like I had a reason to turn him down," Kelsey replied sweetly. "I'm not dating anyone else."

"Some days I wonder if Tyler made a mistake falling for you," Zach said.

"He hasn't," Kelsey said.

"You have no idea," Zach said. "Fine. I'll let him worry. That's what you want."

Kelsey shook her head. "You know what I want, Zachary."

Zach sighed. "I know. I'm working on it."

"Work harder," Kelsey replied.

"You think you have the upper hand just because Alex Carsten is interested in you."

"I know I do," Kelsey replied. "You told me so."

"I know. Don't tell Tyler. He'll kill me. See you later, Miss North," Zach said.

"Nice to talk to you, Mr. Payne," Kelsey said. Zach winked at her, and he walked off.

Tuesday and Thursday mornings became minor trials for Kelsey as she discovered that Tyler actually expected her to wake him up for Patricia's workouts. Kelsey would knock on his door and worry if this would be the day that she lost control and jumped on the scrumptiously sexy just-out-of-bed Tyler Olsen.

Each time she managed to pull herself out of the boys' apartment after awakening him, she wondered what it was that made him so appealing straight out of bed. Then she would gather herself, and go back to the gym to wait for him to arrive. He always did so within minutes, and thankfully for Kelsey, she managed to keep her emotions in check. But it wasn't without serious restraint.

Jessica was standing next to Kelsey, chatting before class on Tuesday. Tyler sat next to them, reading *The Economist*. Ryan walked up and pulled Jessica's ponytail.

"My father wants to meet you," he said without preamble.

Jessica looked at him, puzzled. "Why?"

Ryan shrugged. "You're on the cover of *Celebrity* magazine," he replied.

Jessica looked at him in disbelief. She stood silently for a moment.

"What?" she finally said. "You can't be serious."

"He is," Tyler said, sliding his iPad over to Kelsey. The cover of the week's *Celebrity* magazine was on the screen. Over a blurry photo of Jessica with a ponytail and wearing her pink fleece jacket was the headline,

Ryan tamer! How this plain Jane snagged one of America's most handsome billionaires.

"I'm dead," Jessica said, sitting on the table. Kelsey bit her lip and patted Jessica's knee in comfort.

"You look cute," Ryan said offhandedly. Jessica glared at him. "Anyway, is Saturday okay?"

"Sure. No problem. I'd love to meet the co- founder of Tactec on Saturday and chat over tea," Jessica replied sarcastically.

"We're having dinner," Ryan said, missing the sarcasm. "Do you guys want to come?" he asked Tyler and Kelsey.

"Yes!" Jessica said. "Please, Kels," she added, grabbing Kelsey's hands.

"Um, okay," Kelsey said.

"You aren't nervous are you?" Ryan asked. "Bob's a pussycat."

"He is, Jess. Much more pleasant than my mom," Tyler said.

"Right," Jessica said, unbelievingly. "I can't believe this. I wonder when my parents will call." She glanced at Ryan. "I still haven't told them about you."

"Well, they probably know now," Ryan said.

That evening, Kelsey brought Jessica dinner from the dining hall.

"How bad was it?" Jessica asked.

Kelsey sighed. "Pretty bad," she replied honestly. Kelsey had been besieged by questions about Jessica during dinner. A national magazine had acknowledged the relationship that was under everyone's noses at Darrow, and now it was the talk of campus.

"I talked to my parents," Jessica said, taking the foil off the plate. "They want me to bring him home for Thanksgiving break. They're pretty upset that I didn't tell them."

"How did they find out?"

"Their dental office subscribes to *Celebrity* for the waiting room."

"Ouch," Kelsey said.

"Did Ryan go to dinner? Of course he did, he's used to this," Jessica said.

"He was with Tyler," Kelsey replied.

"What was I thinking?" Jessica said.

"You like him. What's wrong with that?" Kelsey asked.

"Nothing, I guess," Jessica said, picking up her fork. "When do you think this will blow over? Can I go to lunch tomorrow?"

"Maybe on Friday," Kelsey replied.

On Wednesday afternoon, Kelsey and Tyler met to discuss moot court. Tyler smiled. "We're going against Alana Alexander and someone I think you'll recognize," he said.

Kelsey sighed. Alana's writing partner had been Lucas, her ex-boyfriend.

"Lucas is like a bad penny, Princess," Tyler said.

"Funny, Tyler," Kelsey said, without amusement. At least they'd be on the opposite side of Lucas Anderson.

Tyler looked through the moot court packet. "Interesting," he commented. "Our client has accused the other parent of child abuse. That's why she doesn't want visitation."

"Wouldn't the court limit visitation in that case anyway?" Kelsey asked.

"According to the hypothetical, the court doesn't believe our client. The other parent has said the abuse accusation is simply a ruse designed to keep him away from his child."

"Are you sure you're okay with this?" Kelsey asked.

"It's too late now," Tyler commented. "It's fine, we'll get through it. Anyway, I have you."

"Interesting," Kelsey said.

"So in our case, the client's child is ten, and she hasn't seen her father in six years," Tyler said. "Her mother refuses to turn her over during the scheduled visitation times, and the court is deciding whether to jail the mom for contempt of court. Our job is to keep mom out of jail." Tyler passed Kelsey the envelope.

Kelsey bit her lip. She wanted to ask Tyler a question, but knew it wasn't appropriate.

"Ask me," Tyler said. Kelsey looked up. Tyler was looking directly at her.

"I don't need to know," Kelsey said.

"Kels, the reason I wanted to work on this issue with you is because I knew you wouldn't hold back with me. Your question might be relevant to our work."

"It isn't," Kelsey said. She hated how Tyler always seemed to know what she was thinking.

"Ask me anyway," Tyler said.

"Why wasn't your mother thrown in jail?"

"Because my mother has excellent lawyers," Tyler said. "There was always a wonderful excuse as to why she couldn't comply with visitation. The chauffeur forgot to drive me to the airport, the nanny had the flu, she was buying a company that week. I think she and Barry Cinelli made a list and just ran through it every time Chris complained."

"She never accused Chris of being unfit, though?"

"No," Tyler said.

Kelsey nodded thoughtfully. She glanced at the papers. "Does it say why our client thinks that the child is being abused?"

"Our client says that the child acts differently after seeing her father. That's why she doesn't want her to see him."

"What about supervised visitation?" Kelsey asked.

"Our client doesn't want it," Tyler said.

"Doesn't that point to the assumption that our client is just trying to keep the child away from the father?"

"That's what the other side is going to argue, but we need to come up with a reason why it's completely reasonable."

"I'm at a loss. If it's really about abuse, then a chaperone in a public location should be a possibility?"

"Maybe the abuse is severe? Or psychological?" Tyler hypothesized.

"This is why I don't want to practice family law," Kelsey said. "This case is making me really uncomfortable."

"That's the point of moot court at Darrow. It forces you to challenge your preconceptions," Tyler said.

"That's why you picked the visitation hypothetical," Kelsey said.

"I never understood why I couldn't see my father. This is my opportunity to understand my mother better."

"What reason did your mother give you?"

"My mother doesn't give reasons for the things she does. She just does them," Tyler said.

"Have you asked her?"

"Many times. She said it didn't concern me," Tyler commented.

"She didn't really?" Kelsey said in surprise.

"She did," Tyler said. "Lisa Olsen isn't the easiest person to deal with."

"What does Chris say?"

"That my mother is a vindictive shrew," Tyler said. "So basically, he doesn't know why she kept me from him either."

"I admire your willingness to work on this when you're in the middle of their battle again," Kelsey said.

"It's more like my stupidity," Tyler said. "Especially with the deposition coming up next week."

"What?" Kelsey asked. "I thought you filed a motion to quash?"

"The motion failed. Bill Simon called me last night. I have to go a week from Saturday."

"What are they going to ask you about?" Kelsey asked him.

"Lisa says Chris is going to ask about my childhood trauma of living with her. Chris hasn't given me a clue. Do you want to come? It's at Simon's office. Ryan is going. He wants to see what happens in a deposition. He's never been deposed."

"Ryan's never been deposed?" Kelsey said in surprise. She knew Tyler had, and Ryan had been in much more legal trouble than him.

"To be deposed, they expect you to know something. Everyone assumes Ryan doesn't know anything," Tyler commented.

"I guess you have a point," Kelsey said. "Is Simon representing you?"

"For now," Tyler said. "I don't have time to find counsel right now, and I don't want Jeffrey to find someone for me. He's too close to my mother."

"I see. Sure, I'll go."

"It will be fun," Tyler said.

"No, it won't," Kelsey replied. "Is Chris coming back to Seattle?"

"Not for this."

"Are you sure you're okay with all of this?" Kelsey asked him seriously.

"Like I said, I have you," Tyler replied.

On Saturday night, Jessica's room was a disaster. Jessica had been unable to decide what to wear, so six discarded outfits lay on her bed. Kelsey was wearing a black sheath dress she had bought over the summer.

"Bob's not going to care," Kelsey pointed out.

"I don't believe he's as laid back as you guys say," Jessica said.

"Ryan is his son. Trust me, he's about as laid back as you can get," Kelsey replied. Jessica turned. The red dress flared out as she did.

"How about this one?"

"It's fine. So were the last half dozen," Kelsey said.

There was a knock on the front door. Kelsey got up to answer it. It was Ryan, in jeans and a navy fleece jacket.

"Why are you so dressed up? You look nice though," he said as he entered Jessica's room.

"I'm meeting your father," Jessica scowled.

"Seriously, wear whatever. Are you ready?"

"Do I look ready?" Jessica asked in surprise.

"Yes," Ryan replied. Jessica rolled her eyes, and looked in the mirror.

Ryan grinned. "Will I need to dress up to meet your parents?" he asked.

"You're dating the Drs. Hunter's daughter. You might want to wear Kevlar," Jessica replied, fluffing her hair.

"I'm sure they'll love me," Ryan replied dismissively. "Kels, Tyler's downstairs. He'll drive you over."

"Should I go?" Kelsey asked, looking at Jessica with concern.

"Get a headstart," Ryan said. "I'll take care of Miss Hunter."

"It's okay, Kels," Jessica said, taking a deep breath. "I'll see you there."

Kelsey nodded, picked up her purse and a sweater, and left the room.

Tyler was waiting by the front door when she arrived, wearing jeans and a black wool sweater. "You look nice. How's Jessica?"

"A wreck," Kelsey replied.

Tyler smiled. "She'll be fine once she meets Bob," he said. He held the door for her and they walked to his car.

"Did you read the article?" Tyler asked.

"It was awful," Kelsey said. "It made Jess seem like a gold digger."

"She should sue," Tyler quipped.

"Did you read it?"

"No," Tyler replied. "How are her parents taking it?"

"I think they're reserving judgment until they meet Ryan."

"Do they know who he is?" Tyler asked as they entered the parking lot.

"Oh, yes. The receptionist for the dental office has filled them in. Ryan's made quite a name for himself in the tabloids," Kelsey replied.

"I was afraid of that," Tyler said, opening the car.

"I hope they give him a chance," Kelsey said, getting into the car.

"A lot of parents wouldn't," Tyler replied, sitting next to her and putting on his seat belt.

"I'm not sure mine would," Kelsey said thoughtfully.

"Yes, but you wouldn't pick Ryan. For the long-term, that is," Tyler said, smiling at her.

"Funny," Kelsey said.

"I thought so," Tyler said, as he drove out away from the curb.

As they drove across 520, they saw Ryan's silver Porsche speed past. When they drove up to Bob's house in Medina, they saw Jessica straightening her dress, and Ryan leaning against the car.

"She wanted to wait for you guys," Ryan said as Kelsey and Tyler got out of the car.

"Here we are," Tyler replied. "It will be fine, Jess."

"Right," Jessica said, nervously. Kelsey held her hand and gave it a squeeze.

"Let's go, Miss Hunter," Ryan said. They walked to the front door, and Ryan let them inside. Kelsey looked around with interest. She hadn't entered the house when they hung out at the pool last summer. The style was similar to Tyler's house, but the decor was very different.

Where Tyler's house was sleek Scandinavian, with lots of clean lines and light wood, Ryan's was Asian-themed, just like the outside pool cabana. There was a Buddha fountain in the front entry, and large pots of bamboo grew under soft lights.

"Dad, we're here!" Ryan called out. He dropped his fleece jacket on the bannister and ran up the stairs.

"Are we in Thailand?" Jessica asked.

"Charlotte's handiwork," Tyler replied.

"Ex-wife number four," Kelsey clarified.

"Will I be expected to remember that?" Jessica asked.

"Ryan doesn't, so I don't think you would need to," Tyler said. Ryan and Bob walked down the stairs.

"Tyler, Kelsey," Bob said in greeting. "And this must be Jessica," he said, walking up to her.

"Hello, Mr. Perkins," she said shyly.

"Bob. Mr. Perkins makes me feel old," he smiled. "Come, let's have a drink," he said, gently putting his arm around Jessica and leading them to the living room. They all sat on the plush sofas. Kelsey adjusted one of the raw silk pillows behind her back. From the decor, it was clear that the same designer had decorated Ryan's condo.

"So Jessica, I understand that I have you to thank for Ryan's new thrift," Bob said.

"Excuse me?" Jessica said in confusion.

"The biggest expense Ryan's had in months is a car repair. That's unheard of for my son," Bob said, as the butler placed drinks in front of each of them. As always, their favorites had been noted, and Kelsey received her usual cranberry juice.

"Jessica won't let me buy her anything," Ryan pouted.

"I don't need anything," Jessica replied.

"Never stopped any of my wives," Bob said, taking a cashew from a dish in front of him.

"I'm going to New York for Thanksgiving," Ryan said. "I'll buy plane tickets and a hotel room."

"Hotel? Don't be silly," Jessica said, taking a sip of her drink.

"Are you going to New York to meet the Hunter family?" Bob asked.

"I am," Ryan grinned.

"Wonderful. Please send them my regards, Jessica," Bob said. Jessica nodded.

"So when did you two start going out?" Bob asked Ryan.

"January," Ryan replied.

"And I'm just meeting her now?"

Ryan shrugged. "I've dated a lot of girls you haven't met."

"True. And I guess you were in New York for the summer, Jessica?"

"I was," Jessica replied.

"Are you going back to New York next summer?"

"No," Ryan said.

Jessica looked at him. "I'm not sure," she replied.

Bob smiled. "It's a ways off," he said to Ryan. Ryan frowned and sipped his drink.

"I understand from the article your parents are dentists, Jessica?" Bob asked.

"Yes," she replied.

"You read it?" Ryan asked his father.

"I read all of the articles about you," Bob replied. "It's the only way I know what you're up to."

"It was garbage. They don't understand Jessica at all," Ryan said.

"Wait, you read it, Ryan?" Tyler asked in surprise. "You read something?"

"Ha, ha, Tyler," Ryan replied. Tyler grinned.

"I understand another one is coming out next week. *People* magazine called my office for a quote," Bob said.

Jessica put her hand over her face. Kelsey patted her shoulder.

"So are you bringing Jessica to the party this year?" Bob asked, taking another cashew.

"Of course," Ryan replied.

"What party?" Jessica asked.

"The Tactec corporate party," Ryan replied.

"You haven't asked me," Jessica countered.

Ryan shrugged. "I just assumed you'd go."

"Maybe I'm busy," Jessica said, sipping her drink.

"Miss Hunter, will you accompany me to the Tactec corporate party?" Ryan asked her.

"Perhaps," Jessica replied.

Bob grinned. "Tyler, are you bringing Kelsey again?" he asked.

"I haven't asked her," Tyler replied honestly. "I guess I thought one evening of torture was enough. Will you go, Kels?"

"When is it?" Ryan asked.

"I'm sure Lisa's scheduled it for the Saturday after exams again," Bob replied. "She wants you boys to come."

"Sure, if you'd like me to," Kelsey replied to Tyler.

He smiled. "I'd love it, thanks," he replied.

"See, now Kelsey's going. So you have to go with me," Ryan said to Jessica.

"Take a supermodel," Jessica replied.

"I took one last year. She was boring," Ryan said. "Didn't you learn anything from Dara? If you don't go, everyone will assume we've broken up."

"Maybe we will have by then," Jessica said.

Ryan smiled. "I think not, Miss Hunter."

Jessica shrugged. "You've got to get through my parents, Ryan."

"I'll turn on the charm," he replied.

"They can see through charm," Jessica replied.

"Someone's in trouble," Tyler quipped.

"They're going to hate me, aren't they?" Ryan asked Jessica.

"Hate is a strong word. But you have a lot of baggage," she replied, taking a pistachio from the bowl Bob offered her. Ryan sighed.

"At least you know what you're up against," Bob said to Ryan.

Bob looked at Jessica. "You are not what I was expecting," he said bluntly.

"No?" Jessica said, a little nervously.

"Not in the least. Most people are intimidated by wealth. But you aren't. You clearly aren't dating Ryan for his money. So why are you dating him?"

Jessica looked at Bob, then at Ryan, who was looking at her expectantly. She thought for a moment.

"Ryan is like a piece of coal," Jessica replied. "Everyone thinks that they understand him, but I know that there is a diamond inside. I want to see it sparkle."

Ryan beamed, and Bob glanced over at his son.

"Wow," Bob said. "She's a keeper, Ryan."

"I know," Ryan replied.

At dinner, Jessica sat between Bob and Ryan. Bob chatted with her, while Ryan looked at her happily.

"The food is great," Kelsey said to Tyler.

"Margaret made it," he replied. "Bob fired the chef who was here with Charlotte. He mostly eats take-out," Tyler said. "Anyway, my mother's in London, so there's nothing for her to do at my house."

"Why is your mother in London?" Kelsey asked.

"She's decided that to grow Tactec, they need to buy other companies. She's scouting a few."

"Does she ever not work?"

Tyler smiled. "No," he replied. He looked at Kelsey seriously. "I'm sorry Bob put you on the spot for the party. I'll understand if you don't want to go. I know it's a hassle."

"It's fine if you were planning on taking someone else," Kelsey said.

"I wasn't," Tyler replied. "Frankly, I was thinking about how to get out of it this year. But since I probably can't, I'd love to take you."

"I can wear the same dress as last year," Kelsey said. "You don't have to get me a new one."

"You can't wear the same dress. You and Jessica can go to the spa together. Do you think she'll go?"

"Yes, she's just giving Ryan a hard time," Kelsey said.

"I thought so," Tyler said, looking at the three others at the table, then turning back to Kelsey. "Bob really likes her," he said.

"I thought he would," Kelsey smiled.

"Jessica is quite a step up for Ryan. And both Bob and Ryan know it," Tyler said.

"What kind of girls do you usually date?" Kelsey asked, surprising herself, as well as Tyler.

"Smart ones," Tyler replied.

"Not supermodels?" Kelsey teased.

"Smart ones that look like supermodels," Tyler countered.

Kelsey giggled. "I would think that's a rarity," she said.

"I don't date much," Tyler conceded. "But you knew that."

"I did," Kelsey replied.

When Kelsey arrived back at her apartment on Monday afternoon, a magazine had been slid under the door. A note from Tyler on the top said,

Jeffrey dropped this off. I thought you might be interested.

Kelsey picked up the magazine, and glanced at the cover. Between the headlines touting the latest diets and celebrity happenings, was the following giant headline.

Forget Dara Smith. Here's the girl billionaire Ryan Perkins is *really* **dating.**

Kelsey set down her bag and opened the magazine to the article. She began to read.

After a quiet year, bad boy Ryan Perkins publicly went to Instagram last month to announce to the world that he wasn't dating model Dara Smith. Around our

newsroom, rumors flew and heads were scratched.

Why, when Ryan has been linked to various supermodels for years, and in fact is credited for bringing former girlfriend Kimberly Chan to the attention of the media, was he denying a relationship with this unknown beauty? We decided to find out the answer, and it will surprise you.

"He's absolutely smitten. He follows her around campus like a puppy," says an insider at Darrow Law School.

"Ryan would do anything for her," says another Darrow insider.

On the shores of Lake Washington in Seattle, Darrow Law School is known for nurturing the finest legal minds in the country. And after a gap year of partying all over the world, it became Ryan's new home.

Back on his home turf, Ryan was expected to resume his lifestyle of balancing his studies with rowdy weekends, fueled with champagne, beautiful women, and plenty of his father's money. But within weeks of the start of school, Ryan was a different man.

Jessica Leigh Hunter doesn't stand out among her peers at Darrow. A voluptuous, auburn-haired beauty from New York City, Jessica is an average student who spends her days in class and her evenings in the library. When asked to describe her, most people we spoke to knew only one thing about her. That she has Ryan Perkins wrapped around her finger.

"It's crazy. She's no prettier than anyone else on campus, and certainly no smarter," said one student.

"Jessica Hunter? I think you'd describe her as a good girl. She does what she's supposed to do. Except she's dating Ryan Perkins. So it doesn't make sense at all," commented another Darrow student.

So how did this middle-class girl of Italian heritage land one of the most eligible bachelors in the world? Opinions on campus are varied as the students. But one thing everyone agrees on: Jessica is the one in charge.

"Supposedly she turned him down sixteen times before she agreed to go out on a date," said one student.

"Jessica isn't worried about losing Ryan. But he's desperate not to lose her," said another.

As befits her modest nature and his new outlook, Jessica and Ryan avoid Seattle's hot night spots and instead can be found on weekends having quiet dinners near campus, or studying together.

So will it last? Or is this just another in a line of unconventional girlfriends for Ryan Perkins?

One insider on campus thinks it's the real thing.

"Ryan Perkins usually changes girlfriends the way most guys change shirts. But they've been together for most of the year. I can't believe there's not something different about this girl."

And as for Jessica, what is she getting out of the relationship?

When we asked one insider, she laughed at the question.

"He's a billionaire. What do you think?"

Kelsey and Jessica spent Thursday evening knitting. Jessica had finished Ryan's hat, and had started on the scarf, while Kelsey was still struggling with the first half of Tyler's hat.

"This won't be done before next Easter, much less Christmas," Kelsey commented.

"I'll finish it for you if it isn't done soon," Jessica said. "You just have to work on it every night, otherwise you'll forget what you've learned."

"Yeah, you're right," Kelsey agreed. She knit for another few minutes, then asked, "Will the scarf be easier?"

"Nope," Jessica said.

"Thanks a lot," Kelsey commented.

Jessica grinned. "I'm just trying to be honest."

Kelsey sighed.

On Saturday morning, Kelsey joined Tyler and Ryan in Bill Simon's office. Bill was preparing Tyler for the deposition, which was scheduled to begin in a few minutes.

"Tyler, remember to wait a moment before answering any questions in case I have an objection. The court reporter can't write down a nod or a shake of the head, so make sure you speak," Bill Simon said to him.

"Okay," Tyler said.

"And you two, be quiet," Simon warned Kelsey and Ryan.

"I won't say anything. I don't want to miss a minute of this," Ryan commented.

"All right. Let's go," Simon said. He led the group to the conference room, where Lisa and Chris's lawyers were sitting. Lisa's lawyer stood and reached her hand out to Tyler.

"Ellen Tolbert from Collins Nicol. I'm representing your mother during the deposition."

"Hi," Tyler said, shaking her hand.

Chris's lawyer surveyed Tyler but didn't stand.

"Dave Richards," he said.

"Hello," Tyler said, sitting down.

"These are two of my interns. They'll be sitting in today."

"Ryan Perkins is interning with you?" Dave Richards said casually.

"Today he is," Simon said smoothly.

"Fine," Dave Richards said with amusement. "I don't object as long as they're quiet."

"It's not a problem," Simon said.

"Is the stenographer ready?" Richards said.

"Yes," the stenographer said.

"Then let's begin. Please state your name for the record."

"Tyler Davis Olsen."

"And the names of your parents?"

"Christopher Patrick Davis and Lisa Elizabeth Olsen."

"What do you do?"

"I'm a second-year law student at Darrow Law School," Tyler replied.

"Mr. Olsen, the purpose of today's deposition is to ask you a few questions about your childhood. So I'd like to begin with your recollection of the number of times that you saw your father between the ages of three and eighteen," Richards asked him.

Tyler waited for Simon, then answered.

"Three," Tyler replied.

"What ages were you during the visits?"

"Ten, fourteen, and on my eighteenth birthday," Tyler replied.

"What were the circumstances of those visits?" Richards asked.

"Objection, confusing," Simon said.

"What's confusing?" Richards said.

"What are you trying to determine?" Simon asked.

"Why Lisa Olsen put him on a plane."

"Objection, speculation. Answer if you can, Tyler."

"Because she decided to when I was ten and fourteen. I bought the plane ticket myself when I was eighteen," Tyler replied.

"Why were you kept from your father?"

"Objection, speculation. Answer, Tyler."

"I have no idea," Tyler replied.

Richards looked at Tyler curiously. "None at all?"

"Objection, asked and answered. Go ahead."

"No," Tyler said.

"Was there anything that your mother didn't want Chris to know about you?" Richards asked.

"Objection, speculation. Answer, Tyler."

"I wouldn't think so," Tyler replied.

"Did you have a good childhood, Tyler?"

Tyler shrugged. "I guess so."

"How did you feel not having your father in your life?" Richards asked.

Tyler was silent for a moment. "I didn't like it," he finally answered.

"How did you react to not having Christopher Davis in your life?" Richards asked.

"Objection, confusing." Simon said. Tyler looked at him. "Answer if you can."

"I don't know. I'm not sure I did."

"Really?" Richards said, but to Kelsey, it didn't seem as though he was asking a question.

Richards continued. "Is it true that you illegally acquired prescription medication during your school years for your own use?"

"I'm going to object based on privilege. Tyler, don't answer that question."

"What privilege, Bill?" Richards said.

"Doctor-patient." Simon said. "I'll also object based on the fact that your question is calling for a legal conclusion."

"Tyler is a lawyer."

"Tyler is a law student."

"I need to talk with my lawyer," Tyler said, rising.

"Mr. Olsen," Dave Richards warned.

"He's correct," Bill Simon said. "We're going to take a break."

"Stay here," Tyler said to Ryan quietly. "I want to know what he's planning."

"Come on, Kels," Tyler said to her. Simon, Tyler, and Kelsey left the conference room and walked into an empty office. Simon shut the door.

"Tyler? What's going on? What is he asking about drugs for?" Simon asked as he sat. Tyler leaned against the wall, and Kelsey stood by the door.

"When I was in my first semester of high school, I started seeing a therapist. It was why I saw Chris that year, my therapist thought it would be a good idea. When I went to New York, Chris found the anti-depressant I had been prescribed. I didn't want to explain it, and Chris jumped to conclusions. He hadn't been told."

"Why didn't you tell your father?" Simon asked.

"I didn't think Chris would understand, and of course I barely knew him. He threw out my prescription, blamed Ryan's influence, and lectured me about my health for the rest of the visit. When I came back, I told my mother I had lost my medicine, and got a new prescription."

"Did your father tell your mother about what he had found?"

"I don't know, but since she knew the truth, I never heard about it," Tyler sighed. "So what is his lawyer doing?"

"I think they are going to try to use the theory that for at least part of your childhood, Lisa was keeping you away from Chris because you were taking drugs, and she didn't want him to know," Simon speculated.

"Are you kidding me?" Tyler replied.

"I'm not sure why they would be asking those kind of questions otherwise," Simon replied.

"I'm going to have to get a full-time lawyer for this, aren't I?" Tyler said.

"I'll recommend one for you," Simon stood up. "Let's go back," he said, opening the door. Kelsey and Tyler followed Simon into the conference room.

"They want your medical records," Ryan whispered to Tyler as he sat down.

"They can't have them," Tyler replied.

"Let's continue," Chris' lawyer said. "Have you been treated for drug use?"

"Objection, once again on medical privilege. Tyler, don't answer, because we are not waiving your privilege," Tyler bit his lip, but said nothing.

"Have you ever been arrested for drug possession?"

Tyler was silent, but Simon didn't object.

"No," Tyler replied.

"How about any of your friends?"

"Objection, confusing. What's the question?"

"Have any of your friends been arrested for drug possession?"

"Objection, calls for speculation. Go ahead and answer, Tyler."

"Yes."

"There's no speculation, counsel," Chris' lawyer said.

"I say there is," Bill Simon replied.

"So you have friends who have been arrested for possession, and you're hiding behind doctor-patient privilege."

"I didn't hear a question," Simon commented.

"There wasn't one," Richards said.

"Then Tyler doesn't need to be here," Simon replied.

"We aren't done," Richards said sharply.

"I won't allow you to harass my client. Ask your questions or go," Simon said.

"Is it true that your father found illegal drugs in your bag when you visited his home when you were in high school?"

"Objection, calls for a legal conclusion," Simon said.

"Fine. Is it true that your father found pharmaceuticals in your bag when you visited his home when you were in high school? And Bill, there's no parent-child privilege in the Ninth Circuit."

"I'm aware of that, counsel. I'm sure your client would have waived it anyway. Answer the question."

"Yes," Tyler said.

"How much money do you get from your mother every month?" Richards asked him.

Simon nodded.

"It depends. Between five and ten thousand dollars."

Chris' lawyer looked surprised.

"What do you spend it on?" he asked as a follow-up question.

Simon remained silent.

"Various things," Tyler replied.

"Alcohol?" Richards speculated.

"No."

"Why not?" Richards asked.

"My friends don't drink," Tyler replied.

"Do you pay your tuition out of your monthly money?"

"No."

"It's only for your use?" Richards said.

"Yes," Tyler replied.

"What does a young man your age do with so much money?"

"Objection, calls for speculation," Simon commented.

"What do you do with so much money, Tyler?" Richards clarified.

"Objection, asked and answered," Simon said.

"Various isn't an answer, Bill," Richards said testily.

"Ask the question you're dancing around," Simon ordered.

"Do you spend any of your money on illegal drugs? Do I need to define that, Bill?"

"No need," Simon replied. "Answer the question, Tyler."

"No, never," Tyler replied. "Does Chris think I'm a drug addict?" he asked.

Simon and Richards looked surprised.

"I'm asking the questions, Mr. Olsen," Richards said. Bill glared at Tyler.

"Fine," Tyler said.

"I'm going to warn you again about harassing my client," Bill Simon said.

"Thanks for the warning. Tyler, how much money did you receive monthly during high school?"

Tyler thought for a moment. "Three hundred dollars per month," he finally answered.

"Why so little in comparison to now?"

"Objection, calls for speculation. You can answer, Tyler."

"I don't know," Tyler answered.

"Because your mother was concerned that you'd spend it on drugs?"

"This is the weirdest conversation I've ever heard. But I'm enjoying it," Ryan whispered to Kelsey. Kelsey wasn't enjoying it at all. She couldn't believe what Tyler's father's lawyer was suggesting.

"Objection, calls for speculation. Answer the question, Tyler."

"She knew I wasn't," Tyler replied. "So I don't know why I got so little."

"Why do you get so much now?"

"Objection, calls for speculation. Go ahead, Tyler."

"Because I'm getting cut off at graduation," Tyler replied.

"Aren't you working for Tactec after graduation?"

"Yes, but I'll receive a salary in line with other employees. I'm supposed to be saving up now."

"Are you?"

"I try," Tyler replied.

"How much do you spend per month?" Tyler thought for a moment, which gave time to Simon. He didn't object, so Tyler continued.

"About a thousand dollars per month."

"Name the three top things that you spend money on."

"Eating, going out, and my car," Tyler replied.

"And in high school? Your expenses then?"

"Eating, going out, and my car," Tyler replied. Chris' lawyer seemed disappointed.

"But then, Mr. Olsen, we get back to the question of those pharmaceuticals in high school," Richards said.

"That isn't a question, counsel," Simon pointed out. "As I keep saying, I'm not going to let you harass my client. He's answered your questions, and you keep running back to issues relating to Tyler's doctor-patient privilege."

"My client believes that Tyler's history of drug use is relevant to the issues at hand. If Mr. Davis had been involved in Tyler's childhood, he believes that Tyler's life would have turned out differently."

"Tyler doesn't have a history of drug use. Your client found some pills years ago. They could have been aspirin. We have no idea," Simon commented.

"Tyler does," Richards said, looking directly at Tyler.

"Mr. Olsen is a law-abiding, productive member of society. The purpose of this deposition was simply to determine Mr. Olsen's recollection of his visits with his father, nothing more. If you are interested in questioning Mr. Olsen's medical history, then we'll need to talk to the judge." Simon said.

"Fine. Let's do that, because we believe it's relevant," Richards said, refusing to back down.

"Okay, but if you think that you're going to make a case that a Harvard valedictorian and current Darrow Law Student was somehow harmed by not having a father in his life, it's not going to go well for you. With that type of outcome, fathers around the country should be kicked out of their homes." Bill Simon looked at Tyler. "Take a break, you three. We'll call the judge."

Tyler. Ryan, and Kelsey left the room and walked to Tyler's old office, which was currently empty. Tyler shut the door and sat in his old chair. Ryan and Kelsey took the client chairs.

"Are you okay?" Kelsey asked Tyler.

"Honestly? No. I didn't expect this."

"Does Chris really think you were doing drugs in high school?" Ryan asked.

"I guess so," Tyler replied.

"Unbelievable," Ryan said.

"Why is he doing this? Does he really need the money this badly?" Tyler asked.

"Why don't you tell him the truth?" Ryan asked.

"Because it's none of his business," Tyler replied. "It was years ago. Anyway, Chris shouldn't be using me like this."

"Maybe Lisa was right to keep you away from him," Ryan said.

Tyler glared at him. "You just don't like Chris."

"I'm guessing that you don't like him much yourself right now," Ryan replied.

"Good guess," Tyler said.

"Do you have anything to eat?" Ryan asked.

"Check in the kitchen. There's usually leftover pizza there," Tyler replied. Ryan stood up and left the office, shutting the door behind him.

"I'm sorry this is happening to you," Kelsey said to him.

"Wait until Lisa hears about this theory. She's going to go nuts."

"That's right, her lawyer's right there," Kelsey said. "She's been so quiet, I had forgotten."

"If a word of this gets out, the Barracuda will be adding slander to his list of counterclaims." Tyler said.

"Your father can't really believe that you took drugs, right?" Kelsey said.

"I don't know what Chris believes. Obviously, I should have been paying better attention when I lived with him."

Ryan walked back into the office, holding a handful of chocolate kisses.

"Give me one," Tyler said to him.

Ryan tossed one across the desk, and Tyler caught it.

"They're going crazy in the conference room," Ryan said. "Lisa's lawyer is yelling at Chris' lawyer and Simon doesn't look happy either." He extended a kiss to Kelsey. "Want one?"

"Sure," Kelsey said, taking it.

"This is a nightmare," Tyler said, balling up the foil.

"Sorry, Tyler," Ryan said.

"You should be. It's all your fault," Tyler replied.

Ryan laughed. "Technically, I wasn't in possession of anything," he replied.

"Like that matters," Tyler said. "'Are you friends with anyone who's been arrested for drug possession?' He was looking right at you."

"Wasn't mine," Ryan said to Kelsey.

"Doesn't matter now," Tyler ran his hand through his brown hair. "I wonder who my new lawyer will be."

"Simon's doing a good job," Ryan commented.

"Simon's got better things to do."

"Why not just get someone from Collins Nicol?" Kelsey asked.

"Conflict of interest. I certainly don't want to have the same lawyers as Lisa."

"Why not? Lisa won't come up with any defenses that make you look bad," Ryan said, eating a kiss.

"I need my own counsel. I'm not turning over my medical records. I might as well publish them if I do."

Bill Simon opened the door and stuck his head in.

"Come back."

Tyler, Ryan, and Kelsey all stood. Ryan gave each of the other two chocolate kisses.

"Good luck," Kelsey said as Tyler unwrapped his.

"Thanks, I'll need it," Tyler replied.

They returned to the conference room and sat down. All of the lawyers looked angry.

"We're back on the record." Chris' lawyer said to the stenographer. "Per our conversation with Judge Roberts, Mr. Olsen won't be answering any further questions today. We will subpoena Mr. Olsen's childhood medical records, and restart the deposition once they have been received."

Bill Simon frowned.

"We're done for the day. Thank you," Richards said to the stenographer. She nodded, packed her things and left.

"It was nice to meet you, Tyler. I look forward to talking to you again," Dave Richards said, standing.

Tyler said nothing.

Richards left the conference room, and Tolbert spoke.

"Tyler, I'll be reporting this to your mother this afternoon," she said to him. "My guess is she'll want to talk to you."

"I would assume so," Tyler said. "Thanks."

Tolbert nodded, shook hands with Simon, and left the conference room as well.

Simon looked at Tyler. "Tyler, if you want, I'll continue to represent you. This is ridiculous."

"Thanks," Tyler said.

"Did Chris have access to your medical records when you were a child?" Simon asked.

"I don't think so under the parenting plan. He was across the country, so I think that Lisa made all of the medical decisions."

"Check with your mother, okay?"

"Okay," Tyler said.

"I need to ask you a question. Ryan, Kelsey, leave the room," Simon said.

"Okay," Kelsey said, and she and Ryan left the room. They stood by the reception desk and ate chocolate kisses.

"That was fun," Ryan commented.

"It was not. Poor Tyler," Kelsey replied. She threw a foil wrapper at Ryan, who picked it up when it fell on the floor.

"Chris is a jerk," Ryan concluded, popping a kiss into his mouth.

A few moments later, Tyler left the room.

"Let's go," he said to the two of them.

"Bye. Mr. Simon," Kelsey said, waving through the glass wall. Ryan did the same.

"Goodbye, Kelsey, Ryan. Tyler, call me next week," Simon said, picking up the phone.

"Okay," Tyler said. The three of them left the office and went to the elevator bank. Tyler's phone rang as they got to the lobby.

"Mom," he said, picking up.

He listened for a moment.

"No, that's exactly what he's suggesting. Ellen's correct."

Tyler listened for another moment. "No, I think I'm going to keep Simon. He said he'd do it." There was a pause, then Tyler said, "I agree. He'll be fine. He wanted to know if Chris had access to my medical records when I was a kid." Tyler waited for the answer. "Okay. Thanks," and he hung up.

"Well?" Ryan asked.

"She was livid. Now, I think I would call her homicidal," Tyler said. "She's particularly furious because if she sued him, his accusation would become public, and clearly she doesn't want that."

"What did Simon ask you? When he threw me and Kelsey out of the room?" Ryan asked, eating the last of the chocolate kisses.

"He wanted to know if there was something in my medical records that I didn't want released," Tyler said.

"Is there?" Ryan asked Tyler.

"You know there is," Tyler replied without elaboration. "Did you eat all of the chocolate?"

Ryan, Tyler and Kelsey returned to campus after eating lunch downtown. Kelsey spent the afternoon studying, then when Jess returned from a long walk with Ryan, the girls joined the boys at the dining hall. After dinner, Kelsey and Jessica locked the door of their apartment, and worked on their knitting projects. Around 8 p.m., there was a knock on the door.

"Hang on," Jessica said. She and Kelsey quickly tucked their knitting out of sight. Jessica walked over to the door and opened it. Ryan stood at the door. He greeted her with a kiss.

"Hey," Jessica said to him. "What's up? I thought you were studying."

Ryan sighed and sat on the sofa.

"Tyler was just screaming at Chris over the phone," Ryan said.

"Tyler?" Kelsey said in surprise. She had never even heard Tyler raise his voice.

"I didn't know that Tyler knew some of the words he called Chris," Ryan commented. He seemed surprised as well.

"What did he say?" Jessica asked.

Ryan sighed. "Tyler accused Chris of using him to get Lisa to settle. He said that the only reason that Chris is fighting for Tyler's medical records is because he wants to find something to get in the way of Lisa's plan to make Tyler CEO. Then she'll have to settle with Chris. I've never seen Tyler so angry."

"Is Tyler okay?" Kelsey asked Ryan.

"He stormed out. I don't know," Ryan said.

Kelsey bit her lip. "Should we call him?" she asked.

"I tried. He wouldn't pick up," Ryan said.

Kelsey picked up her phone, and sent Tyler a message.

Are you okay?

There was a long pause, then Tyler messaged her back.

No.

Where are you? she asked him.

My car. Darrow parking lot.

Kelsey jumped up and grabbed her fleece.

"I'll be back," she said, leaving the apartment.

She ran over to the parking lot. Tyler was sitting behind the wheel of his Audi. He looked up. Kelsey walked over to the passenger side of the car and got in.

"Ryan told you," he said.

Kelsey nodded. "What happened?"

"I snapped," Tyler replied. He closed his eyes, and sighed. "I can't believe he's doing this to me."

"What happened?" Kelsey asked again. Tyler looked at her. "You were okay at the deposition," she explained.

"Chris' lawyer made a settlement offer. Twenty million and he'll drop the case," Tyler said. "Lisa told him to go pound sand, and when she did, Richards made the comment, 'There must be something really good in Tyler's medical records, are you sure you want to risk him not being CEO?'"

"She told you?" Kelsey said.

"I was on the call."

"Why was she talking to opposing counsel?"

"She wanted to hear the offer herself."

"Tyler, I'm so sorry," Kelsey said. Her heart went out to him.

"I had no idea that this was what having a father was like," Tyler said sadly.

"Tyler…." Kelsey began, then she stopped herself and stroked his hair instead. There was nothing she could say. Tyler leaned his head on her shoulder.

"I never believed her," Tyler said softly. "She warned me that Chris wasn't who I thought he was. I just didn't realize he would turn on me too." He sat up and looked at Kelsey. She rubbed his arm gently. They sat in silence for a moment.

"It occurred to me that you don't know what's in my medical records," Tyler finally said to Kelsey.

"I don't have to know," Kelsey replied.

"It's a secret from the world, not from you," Tyler replied, matter-of-factly. "You know I don't eat when I'm stressed."

Too well, Kelsey thought.

"Not eating is my pathetic attempt to control things when everything else is out of my control," Tyler said thoughtfully.

"My first semester of high school, I stopped eating. Margaret noticed the first day, but Mom said I'd eat when I got hungry. I dropped twenty-two pounds, collapsed outside of gym class, and found myself in the hospital with a tube down my throat, and a psychiatrist. I told him I wanted to see Chris. So Lisa relented and sent me to New York."

"Chris took one look at me and decided that I was doing drugs. He spent the entire visit saying how disappointed he was in me. I couldn't take it. I was supposed to stay for a week, but I lasted three days. When I got back, I didn't want to see Chris anymore. I blame my mother for keeping me away from him, but the truth is after that visit, I didn't care if I saw him for years."

"And you don't want him to know," Kelsey said.

"That's why I didn't want to be deposed in the first place. Although I don't want to admit it to Chris or Lisa, at least four of those ten years, she was supporting my decision not to see him by violating the visitation orders."

"When I returned after seeing Chris, I was sent to an outpatient center for eating disorders for six weekends. Spending the weekend surrounded by girls sounded great, but girls with eating disorders aren't as interesting as one might think," Tyler continued.

"What eating disorder?" Kelsey asked him. She only knew of two, anorexia and bulimia.

"EDNOS. Eating disorder not otherwise specified. It's a fancy way of saying that I don't eat when I'm stressed," Tyler commented.

"I was surprised by the drugs accusation during the deposition. It never occurred to me that Chris would use it against me. But now I'm mostly concerned about my medical records being released. Besides the fact that it's my business, ever since she founded Tactec, there have been rumors in the media that my mother has anorexia, because she's so slim. Eating disorders can run in families, and I don't really want this to come up as an issue for her again."

"Does she have anorexia?" Kelsey asked, then immediately regretted it. But Tyler didn't seem to mind.

"No. She's just naturally thin. Anyway, I thought you should know. This is the reason Zach is always on my case about eating during exam week and why Margaret sends over dinner. It's also why my Mom showed up at the hospital."

"She wouldn't have otherwise?" Kelsey asked in surprise.

"If she hadn't been panicked, she would have let Jeffrey take care of it," Tyler replied.

"Are you cured?" Kelsey asked.

Tyler peered at her. "Obviously not. Otherwise you wouldn't have had to pick me up off the floor last year."

"I guess."

"I'm okay, Kels," Tyler said. "I figure working for Simon was the ultimate test, and I certainly didn't stop eating this summer. Anyway, that's why I'm fighting against Chris. I really hate dealing with this, especially now." Tyler sighed deeply. He looked at the ceiling of the car thoughtfully.

He smiled. "Although, I guess second-year is better than third. At least the editor of Law Review is sane." Tyler laughed. "He won't be next year."

Kelsey looked at Tyler. "Brandon?"

"Brandon didn't run, neither did Jennifer. She's getting married."

Kelsey smiled. There was only one other choice.

"You're going to be the Law Review editor next year?" she asked happily.

"It's the first piece of good news all week," Tyler replied.

"Congratulations," Kelsey said to him.

"Thank you."

"Why didn't Brandon run?"

"Because he knew I wanted it. He said it was because of his Dad, though," Tyler replied.

Kelsey was surprised. Perhaps Brandon was as loyal to him as Ryan and Tyler had said he was.

Tyler looked at Kelsey in the dark. "You always make me feel better," he said.

"I'm glad," Kelsey replied. Tyler surveyed her with his eyes, then looked away.

"Anyway, I'll enjoy the calm, peacefulness of our second year of law school while I can," Tyler joked.

"You should," Kelsey said. She decided to keep the mood light, since Tyler seemed to be feeling better. "Are you going to the Halloween party?"

"I plan on it," Tyler replied. "What will you be?"

"I don't know."

"You don't know?"

"My friend from home is bringing my costume," Kelsey explained.

"I see."

"What about you?" Kelsey asked him.

"I'm not telling if you aren't. You'll have to see," Tyler said mysteriously.

"Okay," Kelsey said smiling at him.

"Thanks for sitting in my car with me," Tyler said to her.

"Any time, Mr. Olsen," Kelsey said.

"You're almost there," Jessica said on Tuesday night. Kelsey smiled at her. Tyler's hat was almost done. Jessica was helping her with the shaping, which was going pretty well to her surprise. Jessica had loaned her a set of double-pointed knitting needles, and thanks to Kelsey's diligence over the past week, she felt confident with her work.

"Next, the scarf," Kelsey said. Jessica had finished Ryan's hat two days ago, and was completing his scarf with what seemed to Kelsey record speed.

"Now that you have the knit stitch down, it will be a breeze," Jessica replied.

"That's what you said about the hat."

"If you keep going at the rate you have been, you'll be done before Thanksgiving," Jessica said.

"I hope so," Kelsey said.

Jasmine and Morgan arrived on campus Halloween night, only a few minutes before the campus party was about to begin. Morgan had been working overtime in preparation for a corporate event that was being held at her workplace on Monday, and she had been lucky to be able to take the evening off at all.

Kelsey was nervous. Against her better judgment, she had decided to trust Jasmine to bring her costume, and now she would finally see it. Ryan and Jessica were going as a King and Queen couple, and she had no idea what Tyler was wearing. She hadn't seen him all day.

Jasmine and Morgan parked Jasmine's car outside of the apartment building, and with lots of hugs and giggles, Kelsey escorted them up to the girls' apartment. She opened the door.

"Hey!" Jasmine said to Jessica.

"Hey yourself. Welcome to Seattle," Jessica replied.

"Love your costume," Morgan said to her. Jessica was wearing a beautiful dark red brocade dress with a sweetheart bodice.

"Thanks."

"Where's the hottie?" Jasmine asked, looking around.

Kelsey frowned. "Later, Jazz. Where's my costume?"

"Yeah, I want to see it too." Morgan said.

Kelsey looked at her in surprise. "You haven't seen it either?" she said warily.

"It's like a nuclear secret," Morgan replied. "I don't have a clue."

"But you look great, thanks to all of your healthy eating," Jasmine said brightly.

"Stop stalling," Kelsey said to Jasmine, who grinned. "Seriously, I've been having nightmares. "

"All right," Jasmine said. She removed a key from her purse and opened the lock on her small suitcase. Kelsey glanced at Morgan, who shook her head.

"I told you. It's like she had classified documents in there," Morgan commented.

"I didn't want you to get cold feet," Jasmine said. She handed both of the girls a small folded piece of clothing. Kelsey opened hers up.

She lifted up her costume, a halter bodysuit with a long tail.

"This is what I'm wearing?" Kelsey said.

Jasmine nodded.

Kelsey looked it over. To describe it as lingerie seemed a bit extreme, yet to describe it as an actual piece of clothing seemed wrong as well.

"It looks like something Kim would wear," Jessica said helpfully, adjusting the crown in her curls.

"Exactly. Jasmine, do you really expect me to wear this?" Kelsey asked her.

"We all are."

"This is my costume?" Kelsey said.

"That and the leopard ears," Jasmine noted.

"Remember what I said about nothing too skimpy?" Kelsey asked her.

"No, I don't remember that," Jasmine smiled.

"I have to go to school here," Kelsey said to her, grumpily.

"You'll look great, North. This was the point of the fitness challenge. To look good in something like this."

Kelsey sighed. She should have known that Jasmine had something like this up her sleeve. Not that there were any sleeves on this outfit.

"I will get you back for this," Kelsey said to her.

"Get in line," Morgan said, looking at her own bodysuit. "At least you don't have to wear bunny ears."

"At least you're fifty miles from home," Kelsey said to Morgan.

"Like that matters. You know Jasmine will be putting our photos on

Facebook," Morgan said.

"And Instagram," Jasmine commented. "But Kelsey has already been on Instagram this fall, haven't you?"

Kelsey looked at Jasmine in horror. She realized that Jasmine must have seen Ryan's post of her lying in his bed.

"I didn't tell anyone," Jasmine said, winking. "But I'd know that hair anywhere."

"What are you talking about?" Morgan asked, confused.

"Nothing. Right, Kels?" Jasmine said.

"Wait until you get married," Kelsey said.

"Your parents will be there. I'm safe," Jasmine commented. "Put on the costume, North."

"Seriously?"

"Let's do this," Jasmine said.

Jasmine, Morgan, and Kelsey each put on their respective bodysuits. Jasmine was dressed as a black cat, Morgan was a pale pink bunny, and Kelsey was a golden leopard. Jasmine surveyed them.

"We look great," she announced. Kelsey sighed and looked in the mirror. She had to admit, six weeks of eating right and exercising diligently had made a visible difference to her body.

"I'll let the boys know we're ready," Kelsey said.

"Hang on," Jasmine said. She reached up and adjusted Kelsey's leopard ears.

"I will never forgive you, Jasmine Jefferson," Kelsey said, glaring at her.

"You love me, Kelsey North," Jasmine replied, blowing her a kiss. Kelsey frowned, and left the apartment. She walked to the boys' door and knocked.

"Come in," Tyler said.

Kelsey walked into the boys' apartment, and almost ran into Tyler, who was standing by the door. He looked at her for a long moment.

"You aren't dressed," Kelsey said in surprise.

Tyler pulled his eyes away from her. "Yeah, I can't go. Professor Janssen wants to talk to me about his law review article," he replied.

"You're going now?" Kelsey asked.

"Right now," Tyler said. He looked at her again, then he picked up his bag. "I have to go," he said distractedly. He walked past her and left the apartment. Kelsey watched him leave as Ryan and Zachary walked into the room.

"Wow," Ryan said. He was wearing his king costume, and Zachary was dressed as a military commando.

"You sure don't play fair, Miss North," Zachary said. Kelsey looked at him in puzzlement.

"What do you mean?" Kelsey said.

"What you're wearing. How can any guy resist that? I should ask you out myself," Zach commented. Ryan glared at him.

"Kidding," Zachary said to him, smiling.

"My friend picked it out," Kelsey said. "Tyler isn't going?"

"Law review. There's a problem with one of the articles, and Tyler's trying to fix it," Zach explained.

"Too bad. My girlfriends wanted to meet him," Kelsey said. "I wanted to tell him, but I guess he was in a hurry."

"My guess is that he knew if he didn't leave then, he wouldn't be able to leave later," Zachary said.

"What does that mean?" Kelsey said.

"Look in the mirror," Zach said.

Kelsey frowned at him. "Whatever. We're ready to go," she commented.

She turned.

"Nice tail," Zachary commented. Ryan laughed.

"After I kill Jasmine, I'm coming back for you, Zach," Kelsey said, walking out of the apartment. She walked back to her own, where Morgan was pinning Jessica's crown into her hair, and Jasmine was adjusting Morgan's big fluffy white cottontail.

"Ryan and Zach are dressed," Kelsey said.

"What about the hottie?" Jasmine asked.

"Tyler can't go," Kelsey said.

"Seriously? We came all this way, and he's not going?" Morgan said.

"You'll meet him at Christmas," Kelsey said.

"No fair," Jasmine pouted.

"Knock, knock," Ryan said at the door.

"Come in," Jessica said. Ryan and Zach walked in. Ryan grinned at

Jessica.

"My queen," he said bowing to her. Jessica giggled and curtsied back.

"These are my friends, Jasmine and Morgan," Kelsey said. "This is Ryan and Zach."

"Nice to meet you," Ryan said to them.

"Hi," Zach said.

"Hi," Morgan said, adjusting her ears.

"I've seen you on Instagram," Jasmine said brightly to Ryan.

"I'm warning you, Jazz," Kelsey said. "I'm wearing your costume."

"You never let me have any fun," Jasmine pouted.

"Let's go," Kelsey replied. The girls put on their fleece jackets, walked out of the apartment, and headed toward campus in the cold air.

"I'm walking in with the three of you," Zach commented as they walked through the back gate.

"We look hot, don't we?" Jasmine said, nudging Kelsey.

"You're engaged," Kelsey said.

"Jim doesn't care," Jasmine said.

"He's hoping you'll wear that on your honeymoon," Morgan quipped. Kelsey laughed.

"At least I have a man," Jasmine said. "Unlike the two of you."

"I bet they'll be able to find one tonight," Zach commented.

Morgan hugged Zach's arm. "I like you already," she said. Zach grinned at her.

"Don't forget Kimmy," Ryan said petulantly.

"I haven't," Zachary said, glancing at him.

They walked into the student center and hung up their coats on racks near the dining hall entrance. Zach offered his arms to Morgan and Jasmine, who linked arms with him. Jasmine grabbed Kelsey's hand and, with Ryan and Jessica following behind, the six of them walked into the transformed dining hall.

To Kelsey's chagrin, and Jasmine's delight, their costumes were the talk of the party. Morgan stayed on the dance floor, as Darrow boys lined up to dance with the tall pink bunny. Kelsey was forced to tell six guys, including her friend Marquis, that Jasmine was engaged. And to Kelsey's amusement, Zachary seemed to have assigned himself the task of shielding Kelsey from any guy who made eye contact with her.

"Tyler's really missing out," Jessica said, as she and Kelsey stood by the bar, drinking ginger ale and watching two guys argue over who would get to dance with Morgan next.

Kelsey shrugged. "Knowing Tyler, he's probably going to be happy once he's solved the problem with Professor Janssen."

"But he can't dance with you," Jessica teased.

"He couldn't dance with me if he was here," Kelsey said. "That's all I would need. To dance with Tyler in front of the law school."

Jessica giggled. Ryan walked over, holding his crown in his hand.

"Are you two having fun?" he asked.

"It's great," Jessica said.

"Where's your friend Jasmine?" Ryan asked.

"I haven't seen her." Kelsey scanned around the room. She spotted her chatting with a guy at least a foot taller than the tiny Jasmine. He reached out and tweaked her cat ears, and Jasmine swatted his hand away.

"Should I intervene?" Ryan asked Kelsey protectively.

"Jazz can handle anyone," Kelsey said confidently.

"All right," Ryan said doubtfully, glancing over at Jasmine again, who was now giggling at the guy, who looked embarrassed.

"We're going to go soon," Kelsey said to Jessica. "Jazz and Morgan have to leave by eight tomorrow."

"Why?" Ryan asked. "They can't have brunch with us?"

"I know, sorry," Kelsey said. "Morgan's got to get back to help set up with a big corporate event being held early on Monday morning."

"Too bad," Ryan said. "They're a lot of fun."

"That they are," Kelsey smiled.

Morgan yawned deeply the next morning, as Kelsey warmed Ryan's scones in the oven.

"That was an awesome party, North," Jasmine said, unbraiding her hair and putting it into a ponytail.

"It was. I thought you said there weren't a lot of cute guys here," Morgan said.

"Kelsey's only got her eye on one," Jasmine said. "The single one with two billion dollars."

"That's what you think," Kelsey replied. She put on a potholder and removed the now warm raspberry scones from the oven.

"Did you make those?" Morgan asked her.

Kelsey shook her head. "Ryan did," she replied.

"A billionaire, and he can cook? Jessica needs to marry that one right now," Jasmine said, as Kelsey put the scones on a plate. She walked the plate over to the girls and sat down.

Morgan took a scone and blew on it to cool it off. She took a bite. "Delicious," she said.

"You should give him the recipe for Ben's chocolate scones," Jasmine said, taking a scone of her own.

"Hey, fit month isn't over," Kelsey teased.

"For me it is," Morgan said.

"Eat a scone, North," Jasmine said.

Kelsey laughed and picked up a scone of her own.

"Aren't you glad you did fit month with us?" Jasmine asked her.

"I actually am," Kelsey said. "Now I can eat what I want."

"Don't destroy all your hard work," Jasmine warned.

"I won't, don't worry," Kelsey replied, biting into the scone. It was delicious.

"I'll weigh you at Thanksgiving," Jasmine warned.

"Before Thursday. Not after," Kelsey said.

"Deal," Jasmine said. "Are you bringing the hottie?"

"Christmas, Jazz. He's staying here for Thanksgiving."

"Darn," Jasmine said.

"You're so impatient," Kelsey said, as Morgan licked jam off of her fingers.

"It's just that I was expecting to see him this time," Jasmine said. "I'm disappointed."

After Jasmine and Morgan left, things felt quiet around campus for Kelsey. With fit month over, her workouts with Patricia were over. Tyler was in his last two weeks of Law Review before exams, and although Christian was no Sophia James in terms of working the Law Review staff to death, there was still a lot to do.

Tyler skipped everything except Professor Surathi's class the week before the Law Review went to press. Kelsey didn't see him in the gym, didn't see him at breakfast, lunch or dinner, and never ran into him on campus outside of class.

"He's never going to do it," Ryan said to Zachary as Kelsey and Jessica sat down at dinner on Thursday night.

"Do what?" Jessica asked.

"Yeah, Ryan. Do what?" Zach asked sarcastically.

"You weren't supposed to hear me," Ryan said, looking at Kelsey.

"Go ahead," Kelsey said.

"We were talking about Tyler," Ryan began.

"And?" Kelsey asked sweetly.

"Well…" Ryan stalled.

"Just tell her," Zach said.

"I said Tyler's not going to ask you out. You'll be married to someone else before he gets his nerve up," Ryan said bluntly.

Jessica laughed. "That's terrible."

"It's true," Ryan said.

"It's not. He's going to ask her out before the end of the year," Zach said confidently.

"This year? No way," Ryan replied.

"What do you think, Kels?" Zach asked her.

"I think that it says everything about Tyler that his refusal to ask me out has become a parlor game," Kelsey commented.

"You have to have faith, Miss North," Zachary said.

"Please," Kelsey said skeptically.

"What makes you so sure?" Jessica asked Zach.

"Miss North is working overtime to upset Tyler," Zach said.

"What do you mean?" Kelsey said.

"Alex Carsten. Your Halloween costume. The fact that he's going to spend a week with you at Christmas. He's going to crack soon," Zach said.

"Not Tyler," Jessica said. "He's lasted this long."

"Exactly," Ryan commented. "Kelsey will have kids and Tyler will still be debating whether to take her to the movies."

Kelsey giggled. "Ryan, that's really depressing."

"I've given up," Ryan said.

"But you haven't, have you Miss North?" Zach asked her.

Kelsey sighed. "I'm trying not to think about it," she said honestly.

"I'll bet you a hundred bucks that Tyler asks her by New Year's," Zach said.

"Never going to happen. Make it two hundred," Ryan replied.

"You're actually betting on this?" Kelsey said in outrage.

"You want in on the action, Miss North?" Zach said.

"No," Kelsey pouted.

"Make it a thousand," Zach said.

"No way," Jessica said.

Ryan looked at Zach with his bright blue eyes. Zach grinned.

"You're on," Ryan said. They shook hands.

"I think you just lost a thousand dollars," Jessica said to Zach.

Zach shook his head. "I have confidence in Kelsey."

"I'm not doing anything different to help you win," she said to him.

"You don't have to. Just keep being yourself," Zach said brightly.

Alex Carsten messaged Kelsey to invite her out again, and once again she accepted. This time, Alex had a surprise.

"Do you like basketball?" he asked, as they drove through the Arboretum on Friday night. Kelsey glanced over at him.

"Sure," she said. As Dan North's daughter, she had watched a lot of sports as a kid.

"Great," Alex said. "I have tickets to tonight's game at the UW. Are you up for it?"

"Of course," Kelsey said. She hadn't been to a sporting event since she had seen the Mariners with Zach this summer. Alex drove them over the Montlake Bridge and parked the car. Then they walked out in the cool November weather over to the Hec Ed Pavilion.

"I should have told you to wear purple and gold. It looks like you're rooting for the wrong team," Alex commented. Kelsey looked down. She was wearing a navy fleece over her red sweater and jeans.

"Who are we playing?" she asked.

"Utah. Don't worry, just keep your jacket on."

Kelsey glared at him. "You must be kidding. I'll sweat to death."

"You know these UW fans," Alex teased. "I won't be able to protect you."

"It's okay. I'll sue you if anyone touches me," Kelsey replied.

Alex grinned at her as they walked into the outside doors of the arena.

"I knew I forgot something. I need you to sign a waiver. I left it in the car," Alex said.

"Lawyer humor," Kelsey said.

"We're full of fun. Did you hear the one about the shark?" Alex asked her.

They made their way to their seats, which were at center court.

"Great seats," Kelsey said to Alex.

"Only the best for Miss North," Alex replied.

"Thanks," Kelsey said, taking off her fleece jacket and draping it over the back of her seat.

"I've warned you. I'm not responsible," Alex said.

"I'll take the risk," Kelsey said to him. She looked around the arena. The crowd was a sea of purple jerseys. Alex leaned back in his seat and put his arm around her shoulders. Kelsey glanced at him and he grinned.

"I was hoping that this would feel more like a date, Miss North," he

commented.

Kelsey laughed. "Not if you keep calling me Miss North."

"Okay. Kelsey," Alex said. "So how's Darrow?"

"It's good."

"You have a break soon?"

"Us and the rest of the country," Kelsey replied.

"Are you going back to beautiful Port Townsend, Washington?"

"I am. Are you going back to Philadelphia?"

"I am. But you didn't say 'beautiful Philadelphia,'" Alex replied.

"I've never been, so I didn't know. Is it?" Kelsey asked.

"No," Alex laughed. "But it's home."

"How long will you be gone?"

"Just a long weekend," Alex replied.

"Will you go back for Christmas too?" Kelsey asked.

"Of course. Uncle Alex has to pass out gifts to all of his ungrateful nieces and nephews."

"Sounds like a good time," Kelsey giggled.

"I'm sure," Alex replied. The game started and they turned their attention to the court.

After the game, Alex and Kelsey returned to his car, then drove to the local mall, which had a sports bar. Unlike the one Lucas had taken her to this summer, it looked like part of a chain, and not like a dive.

"Do you drink?" Alex asked her as they looked at the menu.

Kelsey shook her head. She was deciding what to order.

"Such a good girl," Alex said. Kelsey looked up.

"You think?" she said.

"I do," Alex replied.

"You have no idea," Kelsey retorted, looking back down at her menu.

"That sounds like a dare to find out," Alex said.

Kelsey looked back at him. "Do you seriously want to date me?" Kelsey asked him.

"This is a date," Alex replied.

"I haven't signed a waiver," Kelsey replied, looking back at her menu. Alex laughed.

They ordered and as the waitress took the menus away, Alex leaned back in his chair.

"So why do I make you nervous?" Alex asked Kelsey.

Kelsey thought for a moment.

"I've never dated anyone I've worked with," she replied.

"Have you ever wanted to?" Alex asked her.

Kelsey thought. She had done work-study at Portland State, but she had been too focused on studying to date a lot of guys.

"Not really," she replied.

"Do you want to date me?"

"Like you said, you make me nervous," Kelsey replied.

"That's not really an answer," Alex said.

"Alex, I really can't get over the fact that you were my boss at work," Kelsey said honestly. "I can't think of you beyond that."

"That's disappointing," Alex admitted.

"Sorry," Kelsey replied.

"You have a point, though. I haven't dated anyone at Collins Nicol either."

"No?"

"Have you seen the women there?" Alex said. Kelsey pouted. "Present company excluded, of course."

"Of course. Are you only interested in looks?" Kelsey asked him.

Alex thought. "Yeah, pretty much," he replied, laughing.

"I don't believe you."

"Believe what you want. I'm pretty shallow," Alex replied.

"But honest?"

"Exactly." The waitress brought over their drinks. Kelsey took a sip of her Coke.

"All right. Fine. We won't date," Alex said. "You're a cutie, though."

"Thanks," Kelsey said.

"So, what are you working on at Darrow?"

"Moot court's coming up," Kelsey replied.

"What's your topic?" Alex asked.

"It's a visitation case."

"Family court? Oh, right, I heard that Darrow does non-traditional cases for their moot court. Who do you represent?"

"A mother who won't turn her child over for visitation."

"Really? Did you get a choice of topic?"

"We did, but most students don't," Kelsey said. "My partner is Tyler Olsen and the hypothetical is based on his childhood."

"Tyler Olsen again. Darrow's a really small school," Alex commented.

"Less than eighty students in the class now," Kelsey said.

"How many did you start with?

"One hundred and twenty."

"That's ridiculous," Alex said. "I think Darrow fails people out just to remain exclusive."

"You aren't the only one who thinks that," Kelsey agreed.

"Of course you're at the top of your class."

"Not quite," Kelsey said.

"Close enough," Alex replied. "Remember, I've seen your grades."

"I guess you have," Kelsey replied, taking another sip of her Coke.

"You must study all of the time to get A's at Darrow," Alex commented.

"I study a lot."

"Do you date?"

"Not really."

"A little bird told me you were dating Lucas Anderson this summer. He's was a co-worker."

"I suppose."

"Didn't work out?" Alex guessed.

"No," Kelsey said definitively.

"I'm not surprised."

"Why?"

"I heard that he wasn't such a great intern," Alex said. "He wasn't invited back."

"I heard," Kelsey said.

"You on the other hand, everyone loves you."

"Especially David Lim," Kelsey said.

Alex laughed. "Especially him. Beware, he's finding more terrible assignments for next summer."

"Lucky me. Will Emily mentor me again?"

"Well, if you keep refusing to go out with me, I'll probably do it," Alex said.

"You?"

"Sure, why not? If someone's going to be dropping by my office all summer, it might as well be someone easy on the eyes." Alex smiled at her. "I told you, I'm shallow."

Kelsey was about three days from finishing Tyler's scarf on Sunday night. Jessica had finished Ryan's hat and scarf, and had moved on to knitting an apple-shaped hat for her nephew. Kelsey finally felt like she had the hang of knitting, although she was sure that she wouldn't be anywhere near finishing if Jessica hadn't been sitting next to her during most of the process.

"Kelsey, it looks great," Jessica said.

"Thanks, Jess," Kelsey replied.

"Tyler's going to love it," Jessica said.

"I'm glad you thought of this. I had no idea what to get him for Christmas," Kelsey said.

"I know. I was thinking of baking cookies for Ryan. It seemed ridiculous considering that they have Margaret," Jessica said.

"It's funny though. Since they don't get a lot of gifts, I bet they would like anything," Kelsey commented.

"What do you mean?" Jessica asked.

"This summer, we had a conversation about gift giving. No one ever buys them anything."

"Zach bought Tyler a birthday gift," Jessica said.

"Zach bought Tyler a birthday gift because I told him he had to. Zach had never bought Tyler a gift before."

"Are you kidding me?" Jessica said in surprise. Kelsey shook her head no.

"Wow. That's terrible," Jessica said.

"I guess everyone assumes they're so rich they don't need anything,"

Kelsey commented.

"We don't need anything. We get gifts," Jessica said.

"I know. I was really shocked," Kelsey said.

Jessica was thoughtful. "You must have learned a lot about them living there," she finally said.

Kelsey laughed. "I did. They live interesting lives."

"What was the most interesting thing?"

"Did I tell you about my underwear?" Kelsey asked Jessica.

"What?"

"I didn't," Kelsey said. "I came home one day, and half my underwear was missing. It turns out Mariel's job is to replace worn-out clothing."

"Including yours?" Jessica said.

"I guess so. I got completely new underwear on her next visit."

"That's hysterical," Jessica said.

"The thing is though, things were actually pretty normal, besides Mariel and Jeffrey."

"I'm not surprised. I remember when we first found out who they were, I expected… actually, I don't know what I was expecting. But I wasn't expecting this."

Kelsey smiled. "So are you thinking about living in Belltown next summer?"

"Maybe. Will you come with me?"

"Of course."

"I'm just thinking."

"Sure you are, Jess," Kelsey teased.

"I don't know how I'm going to pull this one off," Jessica said. "My parents would have a cow if they found out."

"They're across the country," Kelsey said dismissively.

Jessica looked at Kelsey. "Are you trying to corrupt me?"

Kelsey shrugged. "I told my parents when I moved into Ryan's condo."

"No way. Really? They didn't care?" Jessica said, stunned.

"Nope," Kelsey said.

"I cannot believe your parents are so laid back," Jessica said. "They trust you?"

"I think they know I'm going to do whatever I want, so they hope for the best," Kelsey said honestly.

"Amazing," Jessica sighed.

"Anyway, it was really fun. Ryan cooked all the time and Tyler worked all the time, but we did some cool stuff on the weekends."

"That's what Ryan said. I was completely jealous."

"You were not."

"I was. That's why I'm staying here next summer," Jessica commented.

"Have you told your parents yet?"

Jessica shook her head no. "I've got to get through Thanksgiving first."

"Nervous?"

"I've never been more worried," Jessica said.

"It's going to be fine."

Jessica sighed. "I hope you're right, but I have my doubts."

"Ryan loves you."

"And I love him. But my parents aren't going to," Jessica said.

"How do you know?"

"Come on, Kels. Ryan Perkins? King of trouble?" Jessica said.

"They invited him for Thanksgiving," Kelsey pointed out.

Jessica shook her head and her auburn ponytail bobbed left and right.

"That's meaningless. They might have invited him so they could threaten him in person."

"Oh, Jess," Kelsey laughed.

"Oh, Jess, nothing," Jessica said seriously. "They are capable of anything. I'm worried."

"It's going to be fine. You were worried about meeting Bob, remember?"

"I didn't know him. I know my parents," Jessica said. "They're going to hate Ryan."

"It's only a few days," Kelsey said.

"I suppose," Jessica said.

"Would you break up with him if they told you to?" Kelsey asked.

Jessica sighed deeply. "I really, really hope it doesn't come to that," she said softly.

"One down and one to go," Tyler said triumphantly, as he sat at the lunch table with his tray.

"Congratulations," Kelsey said to him.

"The celebration's a bit more low-key this year," Zach said, looking around the dining hall.

"I don't care," Tyler said, taking a bite of his sandwich. "Law Review is over for the year, and that's the best thing ever."

"So will you be more like Christian or more like Sophia during your term as Law Review editor?" Zach asked.

"One guess," Tyler said.

"Sophia," Zach replied.

Tyler grinned. "Probably," he laughed.

"You're not exactly easygoing," Zach said, eating a potato chip.

"That's true," Tyler said. "I hope to avoid having people complain about me to the Dean, though."

"Just lock them in the Law Review offices and take their phones," Zach said.

"I'm glad Sophia didn't think of that," Tyler said.

"You should write it down. Make sure you remember it," Zach teased.

"I can't possibly be that bad," Tyler mused.

"You're spending another summer learning Bill Simon's work ethic. You're going to be worse," Zach replied.

"Kelsey will keep me in line," Tyler said to her.

"Me?" Kelsey said in surprise.

"Of course. Your job will be to remind me that I have a life," Tyler replied.

"Interesting," Kelsey said. Zach grinned at her.

"How did Janssen's article turn out?" Zach asked Tyler. "You missed Kelsey's Halloween outfit for him."

Kelsey gave a look to Zach.

"It was fine. I won't be taking his class, though. He's really high strung," Tyler said, taking another bite of his sandwich.

"So now we just have to get through moot court," Zach said.

"How's your drug dealer?" Tyler asked him.

"You're going to wish you had taken the criminal law case after you're done," Zach said. "Don't say I didn't warn you."

"We'll be fine," Tyler replied. "Kelsey, do you want to practice this weekend?"

"Sure," Kelsey replied. Moot court was next Friday, and she was determined to do a good job. Particularly since they were competing against Lucas, who had not only stopped speaking to her, but completely ignored her when she was in his presence. For that, Kelsey was eternally grateful.

"So what have I missed while I've been cite-checking?" Tyler asked them.

"Nothing," Zach said. "Ryan and Jess are still driving everyone crazy."

"It's cute overload," Kelsey agreed. "Ryan's so excited to meet her parents."

"I hope it goes well," Zach said doubtfully.

"We all do," Tyler said, taking another bite of his sandwich.

Kelsey walked into the hallway outside of the moot court classroom with Tyler. Her hair was in a professional bun, and she was wearing one of her navy suits from the summer. Tyler stood next to her in a navy suit. Kelsey glanced at him. Tyler looked great in a suit.

"Ready, Princess?" Tyler asked her.

Kelsey glanced at him. "That would be Ms. North to you."

"Ms.?"

"Sounds more lawyerly than Miss," Kelsey explained. "Anyway, princesses don't argue court cases."

"Good point. Sorry," Tyler said.

"You aren't going to stop no matter that I say," Kelsey said.

"No," Tyler agreed, grinning. Suddenly, two more people arrived in the hallway. Lucas, who was wearing a gray suit, and Alana, who wore navy. Alana smiled at them.

"Are you ready?" she asked. Kelsey nodded. Lucas frowned.

"Of course you are. Ready to deny a good man visitation with his little girl," Lucas commented.

Kelsey sighed inwardly.

"Save it for the judge," Tyler commented.

"I can't believe that you're doing this," Lucas said to Tyler. "Of all people, you should know how horrible this is."

"Lucas, it's a hypothetical," Tyler said.

"It wasn't for you," Lucas said. "How many times did you see your father?"

"It's not relevant here," Tyler said.

"Lucas, lay off. Tyler's the lawyer, not the parent," Alana said softly.

"He's representing her," Lucas said.

"So we can all learn something," Tyler replied. "Lucas, someone's always going to be in the wrong. Just don't take those cases."

Lucas gave him a hard look. "Don't tell me what to do," Lucas said.

"Lucas, what's wrong with you?" Alana asked.

"Olsen always does what he wants, no matter who it hurts," Lucas commented. "It makes me angry."

Tyler laughed. "I haven't done anything. Yet," he added. The moot court door opened and the preceding students walked out.

"Come on, Kels. Let's win this," Tyler said. He glanced at Lucas and they all walked in.

"Never again," Tyler said an hour later. Moot court over, he and Kelsey were celebrating off campus at the pub.

Kelsey dipped a fry in ketchup. "Everyone said for us not to take the visitation case," she commented.

"It never occurred to me that I'd rather represent a drug dealer," Tyler replied.

"They did really well," Kelsey said. Alana had done most of the arguing on behalf of the father, and in Kelsey's view, had been very persuasive about the need to punish their client for her refusal to allow visitation.

"That they did. I had no idea Alana was so well-spoken," Tyler said. "She's going to be a great litigator."

"No wonder Collins Nicol wanted her back," Kelsey said. Of the four first-year Darrow students, only Kelsey and Alana had been invited back to Collins Nicol. Kelsey assumed Lucas and Eliza were looking for internships for next summer.

"She works in what group?" Tyler asked, taking a sip of his drink.

"Environmental," Kelsey said.

"Beats family law," Tyler said.

"I'm guessing you're not going to take family law clinic next year?" Kelsey teased.

"You guessed right, Miss North," Tyler replied.

"At least you never have to deal with it again," Kelsey said.

"Yes. Except in my real life," Tyler replied.

"Of course. Sorry," Kelsey said.

"It's certainly not your fault," Tyler said.

"I know. Have you been served yet?" Kelsey asked. Tyler hadn't mentioned it lately.

"Chris said that they'd wait until the new year."

"That's nice," Kelsey said.

"I suppose. I told him I didn't want the stress before exams."

"Does that mean you're not going to fight the next subpoena?"

"No, but I told Chris that if he served me again before exams, I'd fight it on the basis of undue burden and probably win this time. He'd have to serve me again next year anyway. It's more money in attorneys' fees for him."

"I guess that's true," Kelsey said, taking a bite of her sandwich. "Do you think you'll win this time?"

"I hope so. Lisa said that she'd get a copy of the divorce decree for me, but her lawyer has to negotiate to get Chris to agree to unseal it. Lisa says that she had full medical control, but I want proof so I can attach it to my pleadings." Tyler ate another french fry and sighed. "I have to admit moot court was interesting. It never occurred to me that Chris could have argued that my mother was a flight risk."

"Her company is here, though," Kelsey said.

"Her company is everywhere," Tyler replied. "I thought that was an interesting argument on Alana's part. Not that it helped."

"True. Now I understand better why your mother didn't go to jail. It seemed as though the judges thought that the penalty was too extreme," Kelsey said.

"True. Perhaps if she had left the country with me, they might have been more inclined to jail her," Tyler mused.

"Maybe."

"I'm just glad I can see Chris when I like. Of course, now I don't want to see him." Tyler grinned.

"That's actually pretty ironic," Kelsey agreed.

"It's his fault. Well, I'll see him at Christmas. I'm glad to be staying here for Thanksgiving."

"Will you and your mom discuss the case over turkey?" Kelsey asked.

"Probably not. Mom's obsessed with the Taiwan deal. I'm sure that's going to be our topic for the day," Tyler replied.

"Do you ever discuss anything but business with her?"

"No."

"Never?"

"Not really. She's always wanted me to understand the business," Tyler replied.

"You certainly seem to," Kelsey noted.

"I guess. I suppose it will help in the long run," Tyler said.

Kelsey looked at Tyler, who seemed thoughtful.

"You did good today," Kelsey said to him, changing the subject.

"So did you," Tyler replied, taking another fry.

"It was fun," Kelsey said.

"Fun?"

"I liked getting to argue," Kelsey grinned.

"So do you want to litigate?" Tyler asked.

"Maybe," Kelsey said.

"You should. You think quickly on your feet."

"So do you," Kelsey said.

"I'd rather hide behind a pile of books," Tyler replied.

Kelsey laughed. "You're certainly not shy, Mr. Olsen," she pointed out.

"You don't think so?" Tyler asked.

"No," Kelsey replied.

"I'm shy around you," Tyler said.

"What does that mean?" Kelsey asked. "Are you teasing me?"

"Probably. Should I stop?"

Kelsey pondered Tyler. Dealing with him was so frustrating.

"Yes," she snarled.

"Are you upset with me, Miss North?" Tyler asked her.

"I'm thinking that you shouldn't pester me, Mr. Olsen," she replied.

"Fine. I'll miss you over the holiday."

"You'll see me at Christmas."

"That's true. I appreciate the invitation."

"It will be fun."

"Can I pester you then?" Tyler asked.

"Absolutely not," Kelsey said.

"Then I won't have any fun," Tyler said.

"I'm warning you," Kelsey said. Tyler grinned.

"Sorry. I'm just happy to have a break. No law review, moot court's done. I feel free."

"Yeah, I guess it's really the first break you've had in a while," Kelsey said.

"Thanks to my annoying summer with Bill Simon," Tyler said. "It was worth it, though."

"Because of what you learned?" Kelsey asked.

"That, but I made some money too," Tyler said.

Kelsey laughed. "Nothing for you," she said.

"True, but I'm saving up for something."

"Really? Why?" Kelsey asked him.

"I like earning my own money for things sometimes," Tyler said.

"Like your car?" Kelsey asked. She knew that Tyler had paid for it out of his earnings from working in his father's gallery.

"Exactly."

"So what are you saving for this time?" Kelsey asked.

Tyler shook his head. "Something special. I'll let you know later."

Kelsey looked at him in puzzlement. "Okay," she shrugged.

Tyler smiled at her. "It's a surprise," he said mysteriously.

Tyler's upbeat mood lasted throughout the weekend and through the last few days before the Thanksgiving break. He and Zach invited Kelsey to go bowling with them on Saturday, and Tyler spent much of Sunday studying Securities with Kelsey in her apartment. Monday was an ordinary school day, and with Law Review on hiatus until after exams, Tyler was back to his normal, focused self.

"So are you heading back to Medina for Thanksgiving tonight? Or are you going tomorrow morning?" Kelsey asked Tyler, as class was about to start on Tuesday.

"Actually, I'm staying here. My mother had to fly to Taiwan last night. Her deal is falling apart," Tyler said.

Kelsey frowned. "You can't stay here by yourself," she said.

"Of course I can. I have work to do."

"It's Thanksgiving, Tyler. You can come home with me," Kelsey replied.

"Kels…" Tyler began, but Kelsey shushed him.

"No one should be alone on Thanksgiving. I'll let my mom know you're coming," Kelsey picked up her phone and messaged her mother.

Mom, I'm bringing a guest.

Kelsey's mother messaged back:

I know, Kels :)

Kelsey looked at the message, confused.

"Kelsey?" the Professor said from the front of the classroom.

Kelsey dropped the phone into her bag and looked up. "Yes, Professor," she said.

"So where do you live?" Tyler asked Kelsey as they drove into Port Townsend a few hours later.

"Up on the hill. Your driver knew my address last year," Kelsey said.

Tyler shook his head. "I'm not privy to the security reports Martin gets," he replied.

Kelsey laughed. "Turn left here," she said. Tyler turned the car according to Kelsey's directions and pulled up outside of her house a few minutes later. Kelsey jumped out of the car, and ran toward the front door as Tyler started getting their bags out of the car. The front door opened, and Dylan Shaw stood in the doorway. He smiled as he saw Kelsey, then looked confused when he saw Tyler.

"Surprise," Dylan said.

"I don't have to stay," Tyler was insisting a few minutes later.

"Of course you do. There's plenty of space and tons of food," Kelsey replied.

"Dylan's here," Tyler said.

"Yes, but I invited you. You're staying. Anyway, I'd never hear the end of it if Morgan and Jasmine didn't get to meet you. They missed seeing you when they came to Darrow."

"Morgan and Jasmine?"

"My friends from grade school. The Ryan and Zach of my life."

Tyler laughed. "Which one is Ryan?"

"Morgan, definitely," Kelsey said. "But Jazz is a close second. Please stay, Tyler."

"Okay, thanks, Kelsey."

"My pleasure. We'll have a great time."

Dylan and Kelsey were sitting outside in the backyard a while later. Kelsey's mom was cooking and Tyler was helping Kelsey's dad build a display for the shop. Kelsey smiled at Dylan.

"This is certainly a surprise," Dylan said.

"Why didn't you tell me you were coming? Why have you been so quiet?" Kelsey asked.

Dylan shrugged. "It took me a while to get my nerve up to come back. I'm really ashamed about how I treated you last year."

"Don't be ridiculous, Dylan," Kelsey said.

Dylan smiled at her. "I knew you'd understand," he said quietly. "You've done the work. You know how hard it is to get back to normal. I just couldn't face you."

"Well, I'm glad you're here now."

"Are you dating Tyler?"

"No," Kelsey said definitively. "He didn't have anywhere to go for the holiday."

Dylan nodded thoughtfully. "Where's Jess?"

"In New York. She's introducing her boyfriend to her parents."

"Really? Who's Jess going out with?"

Kelsey grinned. "Ryan Perkins."

"No way," Dylan replied.

"It's true," Kelsey said.

"I'm really out of the loop," Dylan said.

"Yes, you are," Kelsey replied.

Dylan looked at Kelsey thoughtfully. "I'm going back to school in the fall."

"Darrow?" Kelsey said excitedly.

"No way," Dylan replied. "Maybe Seattle University Law School. Bigger, less intense."

"Awesome," Kelsey said.

"I'm deciding between that and going back to school in Portland. But I need your help in deciding."

Kelsey nodded.

Dylan cleared his throat, and said, "Kels, I'd like you to go out with me. I don't want you decide now, but I'd like you to think about it over the break. I've had a lot of time to think, and I've realized that you're the one I want in my life."

Kelsey looked at Dylan with a dumbfounded look.

"I know that this seems out of the blue to you, but I have thought of nothing else since I went into rehab. It really made me start thinking about my priorities, and I realized that you were at the top of that list."

Dylan stood up and looked at her lovingly. "Think about it, okay?"

Kelsey nodded blankly.

"I'll see if your mom needs some help," he said, and he left.

A few minutes later, Kelsey wandered into her dad's workshop. She was still stunned by Dylan's declaration.

"Hi, Kels," her dad said pleasantly. "Tyler's quite the carpenter. We're almost done." Kelsey looked at the detailed wooden display case.

Tyler looked at Kelsey with concern. Kelsey put a smile on her face and wrapped her fleece around herself more tightly.

"It's really nice. Great work," Kelsey said brightly.

"Thanks," Tyler said. He looked at Kelsey thoughtfully, then turned back to the case.

"Will you drive it to the store tomorrow?" Kelsey asked.

"I think so," her father said. "Are you going to come down and decorate?"

"Of course," Kelsey said. "The store needs a woman's touch, and Mom won't be there."

"Your mother bought new tinsel in Sequim. I think it's pink," Mr. North said doubtfully.

"Very cool," Kelsey said. She was glad to be in here. It allowed her to forget Dylan for a moment. "Do you want to come to the store tomorrow, Tyler?"

Tyler looked up at her. "Sure. It's done, Mr. North," he said.

"Dan," Mr. North said.

"Dan," Tyler grinned.

"Okay, I'll pull up the truck and we can stick it outside. Give me a minute," Mr. North said, leaving the workshop.

"How's Dylan?" Tyler asked Kelsey.

"Fine," Kelsey said noncommittally.

"Is he returning to Darrow?"

"No," Kelsey said.

Kelsey heard the truck start up. She walked over to the case and touched it with her hand.

"Where did you learn how to do this? Your dad?" Kelsey asked as her father walked in.

Tyler shrugged in response.

"Let's put it in," Mr. North said. "Can you grab a side, Tyler?"

Tyler took one side of the display case, and Kelsey's father took the other. They walked it out of the workshop and Kelsey followed them into the cold. Tyler and her dad maneuvered the case into the truck, and her father threw a tarp over it.

"Now I just have to remember to drive this downtown tomorrow," Mr. North said. "Thanks for the help, Tyler."

"It was fun," Tyler replied.

Mr. North looked at him doubtfully. "Fun? I think someone's been in school too long." He threw an arm around Kelsey and the three of them walked to the house.

"Finally, a house where men are in the majority," Kelsey's father teased. They were all sitting at the dinner table, passing around Mrs. North's meatloaf, potatoes, and macaroni and cheese.

"Enjoy it while you can, Dad. Morgan and Jasmine will be here soon," Kelsey replied.

Dylan pondered Tyler as he passed the potatoes. "You seem happy," Dylan commented to him.

Tyler looked up. "It's nice to be away from Darrow," he replied.

"Told you," Kelsey said. Tyler grinned at her and took a large spoonful of potatoes.

"How is it this year?" Mr. North asked.

"Better," Kelsey said. "Tyler's been helping me a lot."

"Not really," Tyler replied modestly.

"Yes, you have," Kelsey said. "Tyler got straight A's all last year."

"So I read," Dylan commented. He took some peas and passed the bowl to Tyler. "Are you enjoying your billions?"

Tyler glanced at Dylan in irritation. "No," he replied.

"You're the boy that Kelsey went to the party with last year?" Mrs. North said in surprise. Kelsey realized that her mother hadn't understood that the boy she had temporarily lived with this summer was the same person as the billionaire she had gone to the Tactec party with. Not that Kelsey had bothered to explain it to her.

"Yes, Mom," Kelsey said.

"Oh," Mrs. North said.

"Party?" Dylan asked.

"You were in…" Kelsey began, then corrected herself. "Portland. I went to the Tactec corporate party."

"Why?" Dylan asked.

"I needed a date," Tyler replied.

"Are you going this year, Kels?" Dylan asked.

"Am I?" Kelsey asked Tyler.

"Probably," Tyler grinned. "Do you mind?"

Kelsey giggled. "It's fine."

Dylan looked at them uneasily and ate a spoonful of peas.

Mr. and Mrs North looked at each other.

"So Kelsey can wear all of those beautiful clothes again," Mrs. North said, mostly to Kelsey.

"That would be great." Kelsey smiled at her mother.

"You can't wear the same thing twice," Tyler said matter-of-factly.

"My wife is concerned about you spending so much money on Kelsey," Mr. North commented.

Tyler looked at him. "It's a business expense, Dan. I'm not really spending it on Kelsey," he replied.

"Yes, well, you're a billionaire," Dylan said. "There are expectations. I'm surprised you can take Kelsey again."

"Jessica will go this year too," Kelsey said to her parents, glowering at

Dylan.

"Nice," Mrs. North said doubtfully.

"I really appreciate Kelsey being able to accompany me," Tyler said to the Norths. "I hope that it isn't a problem."

"I suppose not," Mrs. North said.

"It's the corporate world," Mr. North said thoughtfully. "I don't miss that."

Tyler smiled at Mr. North. "If I could get out of it, I would," he commented.

"Be a carpenter," Mr. North quipped. "I'd have plenty of work for you here."

Kelsey laid out towels in her bedroom for Tyler and Dylan. She would be staying in the guest bedroom, since her own room was the only one with two beds.

"Nice posters, Kels," Tyler teased, unpacking his bag.

"Thanks," Kelsey pouted.

"So why is Dylan so upset with me?" Tyler asked her.

"I don't know," Kelsey said thoughtfully. "Maybe because you had a good year at Darrow."

"Good is relative," Tyler replied.

"Better than his own," Kelsey stated.

"True," Tyler said. "What did he do in Portland?"

Kelsey shrugged. "You'd have to ask him." Tyler looked at her curiously. "I haven't spoken to Dylan since he left."

"Really?" Tyler asked in surprise.

"It's true."

The doorbell rang.

"They're here!" Kelsey said excitedly, running out of the bedroom and down the stairs. She opened the door to Morgan and Jasmine.

"Is he here?" Morgan asked. Jasmine looked around.

"Yes," Kelsey said. "He's just a guy," she added.

"Yeah, a hot billionaire," Jasmine replied. "Introduce us."

"I will. Dylan's here too."

"Really? Is he okay now?" Morgan asked.

"Yes," Kelsey said doubtfully.

"Kelsey needs to tell us something," Jasmine said, reading Kelsey's face.

"Later," Kelsey whispered.

Tyler walked down the stairs.

"OMG," Morgan whispered. "Kels, if you don't want him, he's mine."

"Hi, Tyler," Kelsey said brightly. "These are my friends, Jasmine and Morgan."

"Hi," Tyler said, extending his hand to both girls. "It's nice to meet you."

"We saw you on television," Jasmine said. Kelsey glared at her.

"Last year. Tactec," Kelsey explained.

"I see," Tyler replied.

"So, what are we doing tonight?" Kelsey asked Morgan.

"Ben invited us to hang out downtown," Morgan said.

Jasmine giggled. "We told him you were back."

"Just what I need," Kelsey said. "Like my life isn't problematic enough. Fine. I'll get my fleece. Can one of you tell Dylan we're going out?"

"I will," Tyler said. "Excuse me," he said, walking down the hall.

"Oh, he is fine," Jasmine said.

"Aren't you engaged?" Kelsey asked.

"I can still look," Jasmine replied.

Kelsey, Jasmine and Morgan walked down the hill, arms linked, while Tyler and Dylan followed behind them silently.

"So what's going on?" Jasmine whispered.

"Dylan told my parents he was coming, but he didn't tell me," Kelsey said.

"So?" Morgan asked.

"Dylan's decided he wants to go out with me."

"And of course, you brought the hottie home," Jasmine said.

"Great move, North," Morgan said. "What are you going to tell Dylan?"

"I'm really trying not to think about it," Kelsey said.

"That means no," Jasmine commented.

"Yeah, it does," Kelsey said.

"Why?" Morgan asked.

"I like Dylan, but I don't see myself in a relationship with him."

"Why not?" Morgan asked.

"My life is finally running smoothly. I don't want to complicate it by starting a relationship with Dylan."

"What about the hottie?" Jasmine asked.

"What about him?" Kelsey said.

"So you're admitting he's hot," Jasmine said.

Kelsey laughed. "I'm admitting nothing."

"So what's your deal with him?" Morgan asked.

"We're friends," Kelsey said. "That's all."

"Is he taking you to that party this year?" Jasmine asked.

"I think so."

"You're more than friends," Jasmine said. Morgan nodded in agreement.

"Yes, I'm his rent-a-date," Kelsey giggled.

"Make sure you get those awesome blonde highlights back," Morgan said. Kelsey giggled again and looked back. Dylan was still walking behind them, but Tyler had stopped to take a photo of the waterfront with his smartphone. The girls stopped walking.

"Come on, Olsen," Dylan griped.

"Sorry," Tyler said. He put his phone in his pocket and ran to catch up.

"Look at that body," Morgan said.

"He works out every day," Kelsey said.

"How do you know?" Jasmine asked.

"I work out every day."

"With him?" Morgan asked.

"Not with him, but at the same time," Kelsey explained. They began walking again.

"He's a billionaire. He's hot. You see him every day. He buys you fancy clothes and takes you out. Yet you aren't dating him? What's wrong with this picture?" Jasmine asked Kelsey.

"No offense, but I think you must have killed some major brain cells in high school," Morgan said.

"Someone has to be interested in starting a relationship," Kelsey said.

"And you aren't? Are you nuts?" Morgan said to her.

"Look, I completely understand not going out with Dylan. His demons run deep. But Tyler? I don't see anything wrong," Jasmine said.

"Tyler is complicated," Kelsey said.

"Who isn't?" Morgan asked.

"Why do I talk to you two? Look, I'm not looking for a relationship. All I want to do is get through the next two years of law school."

"Then you can be a lawyer and live alone with your cats," Jasmine said. "Have we taught you nothing?"

"We've failed her, Jazz," Morgan said, shaking her head. Kelsey giggled.

They walked down Water Street to the small music cafe. Morgan opened the door.

"Kelsey!" someone shouted. Kelsey laughed happily as several of her friends walked over and greeted her. Tyler and Dylan followed them in.

"Hey, Kels," Ben said to her.

"Hi, Ben," Kelsey grinned. Jasmine had taken Tyler's arm and started introducing him around the group. Dylan looked around carefully.

"It's alcohol-free here," Kelsey said comfortingly. "Perfect for people like us."

"Thanks, Kels," Dylan replied. Kelsey looked over. Tyler was sitting between Jasmine and Morgan on a sofa facing the band area, and they were chatting animatedly.

"Kelsey, how's it been going?" Ben asked her, touching her back.

She turned to him. "It's been good."

"We missed you this summer."

"I know. I was working in Seattle."

"Our busy time. Otherwise, I would have loved to have made a road trip."

"You should. I'll show you around my school," Kelsey said.

"Seriously?"

"Of course," Kelsey replied.

"Will you be back for Christmas?"

"I'm planning on it," Kelsey replied.

"Maybe we can go to the movies or something."

"I would like that, Ben," Kelsey said.

"Awesome," Ben said, smiling.

Kelsey turned back to Dylan. "Do you want something to eat?" she asked him.

"Sure," Dylan said.

"Ben, we're going to the counter. Want anything?"

"No thanks, Kelsey," Ben smiled. Kelsey smiled back and walked over to the counter with Dylan. Kelsey pulled some money out of her jacket and looked at the menu.

"What are you in the mood for?" Kelsey asked Dylan.

"How are their shakes?"

"Great," Kelsey replied. "Vanilla's the best."

"Not chocolate?"

"Get vanilla. Trust me."

Dylan looked into Kelsey's eyes. "I trust you. Vanilla it is."

Kelsey smiled and spoke to the girl behind the counter. "Three vanilla shakes, and three oatmeal cookies." The girl took the money for the order from Kelsey and went off to prepare the order.

"Three?" Dylan asked.

"Tyler," Kelsey said. "Morgan and Jazz are both on diets."

Dylan sighed. "Why is he here?"

"Because I invited him."

"Since when are you friends?"

"He's helped me a lot at Darrow," Kelsey said.

"I bet," Dylan said.

"What's your deal, Dylan?" Kelsey asked. "I've helped him too. We're friends."

"I think he's trying to buy you."

Kelsey laughed loudly. "Are you kidding me?"

"He's come into all of this money, and he thinks he can have whatever he wants."

"You are so off base," Kelsey said. "Tyler doesn't want the money."

"Kelsey, no one doesn't want two billion dollars," Dylan said. "Don't be naive."

Kelsey sighed. "I don't want to argue with you, Dylan," she said, as the girl placed a milkshake on the counter next to her. Two more milkshakes arrived, as did a pile of cookies. Kelsey placed one of the giant cookies on top of the milkshake glass. "Eat," she said, pushing the glass towards him. She took one of the glasses and another cookie and walked it over to Tyler. He was surrounded by six girls, all of whom were vying for his attention. Kelsey handed him the glass.

"Need me to be your date?" she asked him, handing him the cookie. Tyler laughed.

"I'm okay for now, but stay within shouting distance," he replied. Kelsey laughed and walked back to Dylan, who was dipping his cookie into the milkshake.

"Good, isn't it?" Kelsey said to him.'

"Great," Dylan replied.

"How long were you inside?" Kelsey asked, breaking her own cookie in half.

"Ninety days."

Kelsey nodded. "How's Ian?" she asked.

"Traumatized," Dylan said. "I actually feel a little guilty."

"So what did you do for the next nine months?"

"I went to my parents' cottage on the ocean for a couple of months," Dylan said. "Then I reapplied to law school. Then I went back into rehab for two weeks. Since then, I've worked at the office, doing accounts payable for the restaurants."

"Was the rehab related to reapplying to law school?"

"Just a tune-up. My AA sponsor thought it would be a good idea."

"Do you still go to AA?" Kelsey asked.

"Daily," Dylan commented. "Do you?"

"Not since high school," Kelsey said. "I was ordered to go, and I stopped as soon as I didn't have to." She took a bite of the cookie.

"Who knows why I left?"

"Only Jess," Kelsey replied. "Matthew might have figured it out."

"Yeah, I'm sure he did. So I guess Tyler knows."

"Maybe."

"Thanks for clearing out my stuff."

"It was fine."

"I didn't mean to worry you guys. I just realized that things had gotten out of control that night."

"I'm glad you got help," Kelsey said.

"Me too. I should have listened to you and Jess sooner." The band started up. Dylan glanced over, then broke off another piece of the cookie and dipped it into the milkshake. He ate it, then asked, "How was your year?"

"Fine. I did okay, had a good summer."

"And Jess is okay?"

"Jess is great."

"So how is she going out with Ryan Perkins?"

"Don't ask. No one on campus understands the two of them. But it's love."

"Crazy. I can't believe Jessica. Then again, Ryan just got billions too."

"Love, not money, Dylan."

"Right, Kels," Dylan said sarcastically. "That's why all of those girls are around Tyler." Kelsey glanced over. She could barely see him in the sea of girls. Morgan and Jasmine had retained their seats next to him, though.

"Tyler had the advance team of Morgan and Jasmine promoting him. It's a small town."

Dylan nodded thoughtfully. He looked at the band for a moment.

"I really missed you," he said.

"We missed you too," Kelsey replied. "It wasn't the same after you left."

"I wonder if the two of you would have gotten mixed up with Olsen and Perkins if I hadn't," Dylan mused.

Kelsey thought back for a moment. If she was honest, she would have to admit that Dylan's departure had been the catalyst for her accepting Tyler's help, and for Jessica meeting Ryan. So Kelsey said nothing. Dylan looked at Kelsey.

"Yeah, I thought so," he said, drinking the shake.

"We were worried about you," Kelsey said simply.

"Which gave them the excuse to barge in," Dylan said.

"Which gave them a reason to be supportive. Jessica cried for days over you," Kelsey said.

"Really?"

"We felt that we should have seen what was going on."

"You did see."

"We didn't do anything."

"You couldn't have done anything. I wouldn't let you," Dylan replied.

"Maybe," Kelsey said, taking another bite of the cookie.

"This wasn't your fault, Kels."

"I know. But it was still hard," she said.

"Yeah," Dylan said.

Tyler stood up from the sofa and walked over to Kelsey. "Help," he said to her. Kelsey looked at him and giggled.

"Morgan and Jasmine are doing what they can, but it's getting insane." Tyler said.

"I'll protect you," Kelsey said. "Stand next to Dylan," she said.

Dylan slid over, so there was more room for Tyler.

"You aren't enjoying the attention?" Dylan asked him.

"Not really," Tyler replied.

"It must be difficult to be a celebrity," Dylan commented.

"What is your problem, Dylan? What have I done to you?" Tyler asked him.

"Nothing," Dylan said, drinking his shake.

Tyler looked him over, then turned to Kelsey. "What time does the store open?" he asked.

"Ten. But we can go in whenever," she replied.

"Where do you run here?" he asked her.

"It depends on my mood," Kelsey replied. "Sometimes I go to the track, sometimes I run on the street. Do you want to go with me tomorrow?"

"Sure. Six?"

"Seven when I'm home," Kelsey replied.

"Slacker," Tyler teased.

Kelsey giggled.

"I'm going to head back," Dylan said, finishing his shake.

"You are? Why?" Kelsey asked.

"I'm tired," Dylan said. "I'll see you back there."

"Okay," Kelsey said. "Just ring the bell if they didn't leave the door open. Dad's usually up late."

"Thanks, Kels," Dylan said. He reached past Tyler, and to Kelsey's surprise, kissed her on the cheek. "Goodnight, Olsen."

"See you, Dylan," Tyler replied. Dylan left the cafe. Kelsey leaned back on the bar in thought.

"It isn't me, right?" Tyler said.

"No. It isn't you," Kelsey replied.

"He's in love with you, isn't he?" Tyler asked her. Kelsey looked at him, surprised.

"Men's intuition," Tyler quipped.

"Impressive," Kelsey commented.

"So what are you going to do?" Tyler asked.

"Why should I tell you?" Kelsey asked.

"Because if I'm going to have to deal with Dylan after we're back at school, I want to be prepared. We do live in the same apartment building."

"I'm going to tell him to go back to Portland," Kelsey sighed. "My life is difficult enough."

"No time for love, Miss North?" Tyler teased.

"Ha, ha," Kelsey replied. "Funny."

"I'm well known for my wit," Tyler replied.

"Why are men so complicated?" Kelsey asked him.

"That's what we say about you," Tyler commented.

"I mean, I haven't seen Dylan for a year, and he shows up and wants me to be his girlfriend. Does that make any sense?" Kelsey asked Tyler.

"Maybe it does to him," Tyler replied.

Kelsey squinted at Tyler. "This what I mean by complicated," she said.

Tyler laughed. "Do you think I'm complicated, Miss North?"

"You're the worst of all," Kelsey said, pouting.

"Yeah, you're right. Women make much more sense," Tyler replied. "Can I have some of your cookie? I deserted mine over there." Kelsey handed him a piece.

"How do you think Ryan and Jessica are doing?" Kelsey asked.

"Well, Ryan didn't message me to say he was back in Seattle, so maybe it's going okay."

"Jess was really worried," Kelsey said.

"I don't blame her. Ryan isn't exactly a father's dream."

"No," Kelsey replied.

"He really loves her," Tyler mused. "I hope it works out for them."

"Me too," Kelsey said, taking a drink of her milkshake, which was almost melted.

"Have you ever been in love?" Kelsey asked him.

"Me?"

"I don't see anyone else here."

Tyler looked at her thoughtfully.

"Yes," he said. "Have you?"

"No time for love," Kelsey replied.

Tyler laughed.

The next morning, Kelsey met Tyler next to the front door. They quietly walked out of the house, and Kelsey led them on an hour-long run through the streets of Port Townsend. They ran past parks and ponds. Kelsey pointed out her former schools and they finally ended up next to the Jefferson County Courthouse.

"My inspiration," Kelsey said as they stretched outside.

"Impressive," Tyler said. "Have you been inside?"

Kelsey sighed. "I have. Several times."

"This is a really beautiful place," Tyler said, looking around.

"You like it?"

"I do. I missed the Northwest when I was in New York. The fresh air, the mountains."

"Go west, young man," Kelsey quipped.

"I'm here to find my fortune."

"I think you've found it," Kelsey commented.

"Not yet," Tyler said.

"Money isn't enough," Kelsey said.

"Not for me," Tyler said.

Kelsey and Tyler had a leisurely breakfast with Dylan, who was quiet all morning. Dylan decided to stay and help Mrs. North with the Thanksgiving preparations, while Kelsey and Tyler prepared to go to the North Wilderness Store and help decorate for the holidays. Kelsey put her hair into a ponytail, and put on jeans and a long sleeved t-shirt, which she then covered with a warm sweater and her fleece jacket. She met Tyler by the front door, and they headed out. Kelsey stuck her hands into her jacket pockets. It was surprisingly cold.

"Would holding your hand be being complicated?" Tyler asked her as they walked down the street.

Kelsey glanced at him. "Not only that, but it would start rumors. This is a small town, Tyler," she replied.

Tyler looked thoughtful. "I can't have any fun with you," he commented.

"Why are you annoying me?" Kelsey asked him.

Tyler smiled. "Am I?" he asked.

"You know that you are," Kelsey said.

"I guess," Tyler replied. "It's just nice to be here with you."

"Is it?" Kelsey teased.

"You know that it is," Tyler said.

Kelsey grinned. "I'm glad that you came with me."

"Me, too," Tyler said. "It's interesting to see where Kelsey North got her start."

"Are you learning anything about me?" Kelsey asked.

"A lot," Tyler said.

"Really?" Kelsey said doubtfully. "Like what?"

Tyler thought for a moment as they headed down the hill. "You're a lot like your Dad. Very direct," he commented.

"That's true," Kelsey said. "I'm nothing like my mother at all."

"You look a little like her."

"A little," Kelsey said, wrinkling her nose.

"Kelsey Anne North, do you not get along with your mother?" Tyler teased.

"I'm a tad upset with her, right now," Kelsey replied.

"I see," Tyler said.

"But, yes, I generally don't get along with her that well," Kelsey replied. "She and I have very different views of what's appropriate."

"Yours are a bit more expansive?" Tyler guessed.

"Exactly. She'd like me to be married, have some grandkids, and stop wasting my time with this lawyer thing," Kelsey said.

"Why is that? You're going to be really successful."

"Thanks. She thinks I'm too headstrong. And I probably am," Kelsey added.

"It's one of your best qualities," Tyler commented.

"One of the best, and one of the worst. She's lived through the worst, so that's what she focuses on," Kelsey said. "My father's a bit more forgiving."

"You haven't been the ideal daughter?" Tyler guessed.

"No," Kelsey replied. "My mother needed a daughter like Jasmine. A pleasant, peaceful carbon copy of her mom. But she got me."

"She's lucky," Tyler said. "She's probably grown from the experience of having you challenge her beliefs."

"I'm not sure she's interested in that kind of personal growth."

"Oh, well. You don't get to choose your children."

"That's for sure," Kelsey noted. "Otherwise, she probably would have returned me."

Tyler smiled. "Your relationship sounds like Lisa's with my grandmother."

"Seriously? She wanted your mother to stay home and be a housewife?"

"She did. In fact, I think she still does."

"That's crazy," Kelsey said. "No offense."

"None taken. I think it's crazy too," Tyler said. He paused, then said, "Sometimes you remind me of my mother."

"Really? How?" Kelsey asked.

"You both very clearly know what you want, and you're determined to get it. Nothing is going to stand in your way."

"I'm honored, but I imagine that your mother is slightly more determined than me."

"I think she just has more practice," Tyler commented.

"Interesting," Kelsey said.

"Your accomplishments are coming, Kelsey. Just wait," Tyler said.

They walked into the store, where Kelsey's father was straightening the display counter. The store was otherwise empty, as expected. Most of the potential shoppers were probably at home, like Mrs. North, preparing for the holiday.

"Hi, Dad."

"Hey, Kels, Tyler. Ready to work?"

"Sure," Kelsey said. "Where's the tinsel?" she asked.

Kelsey and Tyler spent the rest of the morning decorating the store from ceiling to floor. They walked across the street and had pizza, then returned and helped Mr. North put out new stock.

"It looks great," Kelsey proclaimed at six p.m., surveying the store. Tyler, who was tightening a screw on a display rack, nodded.

"It does," Mr. North said. "There's a bit less bling than last year."

"Well, Tyler's here instead of Jessica," Kelsey commented.

"Oh, that's why. Tyler, you'll have to come back every year," Mr. North said.

"What happened with Jess?" Tyler asked, standing and putting the screwdriver on the display counter.

"Let's just say it was very, very sparkly," Mr. North said.

"It was beautiful," Kelsey pouted.

"Of course it was, dear," Mr. North smiled. He looked at his phone. "Where are your mother and Dylan? I'm ready to eat."

"Me, too," Kelsey said. "Where are we going?"

"Mexican? What do you think, Tyler?" Mr. North said.

"Mexican's great," he replied. The bell on the door rang and Dylan and Mrs. North walked in, laughing.

"Oh, it looks beautiful," Mrs. North said in delight.

"Thanks," Mr. North said.

"Like you did any of it," Mrs. North teased.

"I supervised," Mr. North replied. "Are you two ready? We have three votes for Mexican."

"I guess you win then. We were thinking Thai," Mrs. North said.

"We ate a lot of Thai this summer," Kelsey commented, as they walked outside and Mr. North turned off the lights and locked the door of the store.

"We?" Dylan asked.

"Me and Tyler. Ryan learned how to cook, and Thai was a favorite for him to practice with," Kelsey said.

"Your Mom and I will drive," Mr. North said. "Anyone want a ride?"

Kelsey shook her head. "We'll walk, Dad."

"Okay, see you there," Mr. North said. He and Mrs. North headed to the parking lot, while Kelsey, Tyler, and Dylan began walking down Water Street.

"You hung out with Tyler and Ryan?" Dylan said.

"We all worked downtown," Kelsey said. She neglected to mention that she had lived with them. Although her parents knew, she was a little concerned about Dylan's reaction.

"Someone hired Ryan Perkins?" Dylan said. "Oh, of course, he must have worked for Tactec."

"He got an A last term," Kelsey said.

"In what?"

"Constitutional law," Kelsey replied.

"Did he pay someone off?" Dylan asked.

"Ha, ha," Kelsey said, "Not funny, Dylan."

"Just saying," Dylan commented. "How can Jessica date him? I thought she was smart."

"She is," Kelsey said. She glanced at Tyler, who was walking with them, but wasn't paying attention. He was looking at the various storefronts.

"I wonder," Dylan said. "How was your job?"

"Great," Kelsey said. "I'm going back next summer."

"How about you, Tyler? Did you work for Tactec too?"

Tyler looked at Dylan. "What? Sorry," he said. Tyler clearly hadn't been listening to the conversation.

"I asked if you worked for your mother," Dylan said.

"No," Tyler said crisply.

"Where did you work?"

"Simon and Associates," Tyler replied.

"Do they do a lot of work for Tactec?" Dylan asked.

"Actually, they do none. That's why I went there," Tyler replied.

"Didn't want any more undeserved favors? Two billion of them are enough?" Dylan asked.

"You're really in fine form, Dylan," Tyler said. "Did you work on your jokes while you were away from Darrow?"

Dylan gave him a hard look. "It's none of your business what I did while I was away from Darrow."

"Then it's none of your business about what I did this summer," Tyler said. "Or why I did it."

"Fine. I don't need to know." Dylan shrugged.

"Then don't ask," Tyler replied.

"Oh, this is fun," Kelsey said, frowning at Dylan.

"You invited him," Dylan said.

"I mean you," Kelsey said.

"I'm just making conversation," Dylan said.

"Converse about something else," Kelsey replied.

The group was silent as they walked into the restaurant. Mr. and Mrs. North were already sitting at a back table, sharing a bowl of chips and salsa.

"So are we all ready for tomorrow's feast?" Mr. North asked, passing the chips across the table.

"We're ready," Mrs. North said. "Dylan was really helpful. I made him go to the store twice."

"It was my pleasure," Dylan said. Kelsey took a chip and ate it.

The server arrived with menus, which each of them took.

"What are you in the mood for?" Kelsey asked Tyler.

"Everything looks good," Tyler said.

"I know. And I'm starving," Kelsey said.

The waiter came by and they ordered. Mrs. North looked at Tyler. "This must feel very low key for you, Tyler?" she asked him.

Tyler looked up. "I'm sorry, Mrs. North. What do you mean?"

"Well, I imagine your holidays are usually much more exotic than this," she commented.

"Not really," Tyler said.

"Oh, come on. You're a billionaire," Dylan commented.

"In stock only, Dylan. I actually don't travel a lot, Mrs. North," Tyler said.

Mrs. North wrinkled her brow. Kelsey frowned. She wanted her mother to end this topic, but she knew the look on her mother's face all too well. It was full steam ahead.

"Really? I have trouble believing that," Mrs. North commented. Kelsey saw her father frown too. Mrs. North could be very persistent when she thought she was right.

"Everyone knows Ryan Perkins took a trip around the world before Darrow," Dylan said. "You didn't go with him?"

"I was working," Tyler said.

"Right," Dylan said with sarcasm. "For minimum wage?"

"I worked for my father, Dylan," Tyler said.

"Is he a billionaire too?" Dylan asked.

"Far from it," Tyler replied.

"Didn't you go to Europe after graduation?" Kelsey asked Dylan sweetly. She hoped a reminder of his own relative wealth might move them away from the topic.

"For a couple of weeks," Dylan said.

"I've never been," Kelsey continued. "What was your favorite place?"

"Paris, but I'm sure Tyler's much better acquainted with Europe," Dylan said.

Kelsey sighed as their drinks arrived. Tyler glanced at Dylan, but said nothing more.

"So what do you usually do for the holidays?" Mrs. North asked.

"Sit at home," Tyler replied honestly, looking at her.

"Tyler's parents work a lot," Kelsey said to her mother, glaring at her.

"Oh," Mrs. North said chagrined. Kelsey hoped that answer would satisfy her mother.

"Well, I'm sure you'll all travel a lot once you're lawyers," Mr. North said peacefully.

"Probably," Kelsey agreed.

The group sat quietly, eating chips and salsa for a few moments. Kelsey hoped her mother was done with quizzing Tyler. Kelsey wasn't sure what Mrs. North was trying to prove, but she was sure she wouldn't like it.

The food arrived and everyone was served. Kelsey dove into her fajitas.

"It's good," Tyler said to her.

"Better than the place near campus," Kelsey commented.

"I agree," Tyler replied. Mrs. North and Dylan looked at each other.

"There's a lot of new places in Portland to take you to, Kelsey," Dylan said.

"Really?" Kelsey said.

"Yeah, you should come down," Dylan said. "You can stay with us."

"Thanks," Kelsey said.

"How nice," Mrs. North said.

"Generous," Tyler said, quietly.

Dylan glared at him. "Portland's certainly more interesting than Medina," Dylan said.

"That's absolutely true, Dylan," Tyler said.

"Although I'm sure my house isn't as fabulous as yours," Dylan added.

"Well, Kelsey's been to my house. What do you think, Kels?" Tyler asked her.

"They're both lovely," Kelsey commented diplomatically.

"You've been to Tyler's house?" her mother said.

229

"Yes," Kelsey said. "So?"

"I'm just surprised, that's all," Mrs. North said. Kelsey frowned again.

"She's even met my mother," Tyler said, taunting Dylan.

"Why?" Mrs. North asked.

Kelsey shrugged. "She was there."

Mrs. North bit her lip, but said nothing more at dinner.

"Kelsey," Mrs. North said. Tyler, Dylan, and Mr. North had gone downstairs to watch television, and Kelsey was about to join them when her mother spoke.

"Yes?"

"I thought you and Tyler weren't dating," she said.

"We aren't," Kelsey replied.

"But you've met his mother?"

"Sure," Kelsey said.

"Why?"

"I told you. Because she was there. I met her at the party, I've had dinner at their house, she's dropped by school." Kelsey shrugged.

"I'm not sure I realized that you spent so much time with him," Kelsey's mother said.

"Well, I did live with him last summer," Kelsey commented.

"Yes, I know, for about a month. But…" Mrs. North said. "I didn't realize that you had met his family."

"It isn't a big deal," Kelsey said.

"No?"

"No. Jessica's met his mother too. We're classmates. Sometimes parents drop by," Kelsey said. "What's the big deal?"

"I'm just concerned."

"About what?"

"About you getting serious about someone like him," Mrs. North said.

"Like him?" Kelsey asked.

"Someone so different than us," Mrs. North explained.

"What does that mean?"

Mrs. North sighed. "Kelsey, he's a billionaire. Do you really think he lives like we do?"

"I know he doesn't. But that's okay."

"That's okay? You really think that someone with a billion dollars can bring someone normal into their lives?"

"I don't know," Kelsey said honestly. "But it isn't an issue now. We're just friends."

"I think you should think about this."

"Think about what? Being friends with Tyler?" Kelsey asked.

"Getting close to him," her mother said.

"It's a little late for that. I sat next to him all of last year," Kelsey commented.

"You know what I mean, Kelsey Anne," her mother said.

"Why is Dylan different? His family has money. Plenty of it."

"Dylan is normal."

"So is Tyler. You just don't know him."

"Really? It's normal to have friends in the tabloids?"

Kelsey looked at her mother. "It seems to me that Jessica was on the cover of one."

"That's because she's dating Tyler's billionaire friend. Otherwise, she wouldn't be," Mrs. North said. Clearly, Dylan had filled her mother in on the friendship between Tyler and Ryan.

"I really don't know why we're discussing this," Kelsey said.

"Because I think it's important," Mrs. North said sharply.

"Because you like Dylan."

"Because I don't want my daughter to get hurt."

"I can take care of myself," Kelsey said.

"I've heard that before," Mrs. North said disdainfully.

Kelsey bit her lip.

"Mom, what do you want me to say?" Kelsey finally asked her.

"I want you to think about what you're getting into."

"Fine. I'll think about that, whatever that is," Kelsey said in exasperation.

Her mother sighed. "You're so stubborn. You always have been."

"Yep," Kelsey agreed.

"That's why you had so many problems as a child," her mother continued.

"Is it?" Kelsey commented.

Her mother frowned. "Don't be smart with me, Kelsey Anne North. I might have learned something over the past few decades."

"Do you know a lot of billionaires?" Kelsey asked.

"What did I tell you about being smart with me?" Mrs. North said.

"Sorry," Kelsey said, without meaning it.

"You really try my patience," Mrs. North said. "Do what you want to. You always have."

"True," Kelsey said. "And I've accepted the consequences," she noted.

"You've been lucky. I hope you remain so," her mother commented.

"Me too," Kelsey said. She looked at her mother, then left the room.

Kelsey woke up grumpy the next morning, but she took a long hot shower and decided to put on a brave face. It was Thanksgiving, and they had guests to entertain. And at least one of them was hers.

Kelsey walked into the kitchen.

"Do you need help?" Kelsey asked her Mom.

"Not really. Dylan's been helping me this morning," her mother replied. "I'm almost done. Actually, Dylan, if you want to leave and spend time with Kelsey, go ahead."

"Sounds great, Kelly," Dylan said, smiling at Kelsey.

Kelsey walked out of the kitchen with Dylan following her. She went into the living room and sat in a chair. She hung her legs over the side of the arm of the chair.

"Where's Olsen?" Dylan asked her, as he sat on the sofa.

"He drove to the store with Dad. I think they're building another display," Kelsey replied.

Dylan nodded. "So did you think about what I said?"

"I did," Kelsey replied. She sighed. She didn't really want to have this discussion on Thanksgiving, but there it was.

"And?"

"Dylan, you and I are not meant to be together," Kelsey said, bluntly. "You know it and so do I."

"What do you mean?"

"I've known you for years. Why am I suddenly attractive to you?" Kelsey asked him.

"Because you understand me," Dylan said.

Kelsey looked at him. "Is this what this is about? That you're rebuilding your life, and you think I can help you?" Kelsey said.

"That hurts," Dylan said. "It isn't about that. I'm not looking for a shortcut, and I certainly don't need your help."

"Okay, then what is it?"

"I love you."

"No, you don't," Kelsey said. "You're scared. I understand, I've been there. But getting involved with me isn't going to make staying sober easier for you."

"Why don't you believe that I want you?"

"Honestly? Because you never have," Kelsey said.

"I was wrong," Dylan said.

"I don't think you were," Kelsey replied.

"You don't love me?"

"You know that I do. You're one of my best friends. But we aren't going to go beyond that."

"Are you in love with Tyler?" Dylan asked her sharply.

Kelsey took a deep breath. "Tyler has nothing to do with this."

"No, he has everything to do with this," Dylan replied hotly. He stood.

"Dylan. I don't want to fight with you," Kelsey said.

"Look, Kels. Just be honest with me. If you're refusing me because you're in love with Tyler, tell me."

"I'm refusing because it's the right thing to do," Kelsey said. "You're looking for a life raft, now that the alcohol is gone. You get involved with me, you can pretend that it's over, that you're cured. But trust me, it will all come back to bite you."

"Like you're an expert," Dylan snapped.

"It's never over, Dylan. Every day, for the rest of your life, you're going to have to fight. I'd only be a distraction," Kelsey said.

"I hate you," Dylan said, and he left the room.

A half hour later, Tyler and Mr. North walked into the house. Kelsey looked up from her Kindle.

"It's freezing out there," Mr. North said, rubbing his hands together. "Is dinner almost ready?"

"Almost," Kelsey said.

"Why aren't you helping your mother?" Mr. North asked.

"She said she didn't need help," Kelsey replied.

"You should help her anyway," Mr. North said.

"Dad, you know how Mom is during Thanksgiving," Kelsey said in her own defense.

"Cranky," Mr. North agreed. He looked at Tyler. "If we don't have twenty side dishes, it's not Thanksgiving."

"Can I see if she needs help?" Tyler asked.

"Straight into the lion's den," Kelsey said.

"I'll be brave," Tyler said, walking into the kitchen.

"Where's Dylan?" Mr. North asked Kelsey.

Kelsey shrugged.

"You aren't entertaining your guest."

"Dylan's not exactly my guest," Kelsey replied.

Her father smiled. "I suppose not," he said, sitting on the sofa.

"Where were you?" she asked.

"Tyler helped me build the new shoe display," Mr. North said.

"I'm not entertaining the guests, but you're putting them to work," Kelsey noted.

"He's enjoying it," Mr. North said. "It's not everyday you get to use power tools."

"Man stuff," Kelsey said.

"Exactly," Mr. North replied.

"You should have had a son," Kelsey said.

"No, I'm happy to have you," Mr. North said. He took off his jacket and laid it next to him on the sofa.

"Do you think the store will be busy tomorrow?" Kelsey asked.

"I think so. But you kids don't need to come. Have fun with your friends," Mr. North said. "I'll put you to work at Christmas break."

Kelsey laughed. "Okay."

"Tyler's coming for Christmas too, right?"

"He is," Kelsey said. "His mom's working. He'll go to his Dad's house on Christmas Day."

Mr. North nodded. "Why Christmas Day?"

"I don't think he really enjoys the holiday much," Kelsey said.

"Why?"

"His mom always works through it," Kelsey replied.

"We'll be working a lot the week before," Mr. North said.

"Yeah, but we have fun," Kelsey said.

"I suppose that's true."

"Don't worry, I'll make sure we do some traditional Christmas stuff too. Let's make sure we cut down a tree. I think Tyler would like that," Kelsey said.

"Probably," Mr. North said. "It was nice for you to invite him."

"People shouldn't be alone for the holidays," Kelsey commented.

"I agree. It's a shame that he's missed out on the holidays with his family," Mr. North said.

"I suppose that's what happens when your parents run a multi-billion dollar conglomerate," Kelsey said.

"As opposed to a multi-hundred dollar one," Mr. North replied.

"I prefer ours," Kelsey said.

"Me too," Mr. North said.

Mrs. North walked into the room. "Dinner's ready," she said wearily.

"Where's Dylan?" Kelsey asked her.

"He and Tyler are in the kitchen. Why aren't you?" her mother said.

"You said you didn't need any help."

"Kelsey, that's what people say."

"You're my mother. I took you at your word," Kelsey said.

Her mother laughed. "Kelsey Anne North, get up and help your guests."

"Okay," Kelsey said, putting her Kindle aside and standing. She walked into the kitchen. Tyler and Dylan were on opposite sides of the room. Tyler was putting cranberry sauce into a glass bowl, while Dylan was rinsing a dish.

"Need any help?" Kelsey asked.

"I think we have it under control," Tyler said, winking at her.

Dylan was silent.

Kelsey observed him, as Tyler turned back to the cranberry sauce.

"Can I start carrying things to the table, Dylan?" she asked.

"Go ahead," Dylan said coldly. Tyler glanced at him.

"I'll help you," Tyler said to Kelsey. He carried the glass dish of cranberry sauce over to her, and took another dish off of the table. Kelsey led the way to the dining room, carrying a dish of mashed potatoes, and Tyler followed.

"You told him?" Tyler asked her quietly.

"I did. No need to drag it out," Kelsey replied.

"When you can ruin the weekend," Tyler teased.

Kelsey grinned. "Exactly." They went back into the kitchen, grabbed more dishes, and took them into the dining room. They continued carrying dishes into the dining room until everything was on the table. Dylan ignored them, and continued to slowly wash the few dishes that were left. On their last trip into the dining room, Kelsey stuck her head into the living room, where her mother was resting her head on Mr. North's shoulder.

"We're all set," Kelsey said.

"Wash up and let's eat," Mr. North said.

"See you in there," Kelsey said. She and Tyler walked back into the kitchen. Dylan was gone.

"I'll let him know we're ready," Tyler said.

"Thanks," Kelsey replied.

Tyler ran up the stairs and Kelsey followed behind him slowly. She went into the guest room and changed shirts. When she walked past her own room, she heard Dylan's angry voice. She refrained from knocking, and went to the bathroom to wash her hands. When she returned, the door was open and the boys were gone. She went down to the table, and Tyler and Dylan were sitting on opposite sides. Tyler looked up at her, and she rolled her eyes and shook her head. He grinned. Kelsey sat down next to him as her parents walked in. They sat at the table.

"As has become our tradition when we have guests, let's go around the table and say what we're grateful for this year. I'll begin. I'm grateful that we're here together and that Kelsey has brought me two people who'll want to watch the Seahawks play in an hour and a half."

"Dan," Kelsey's mom said lovingly.

"Your turn," he replied.

"I'm grateful to have Kelsey home, to have her dear friend Dylan back, and for us to meet her new friend Tyler."

Kelsey bristled, just a little, at her mother's characterization of Tyler as a new friend. Although he might be new to her parents, he certainly wasn't new to Kelsey.

"Kelsey?" Mrs. North said.

"I'm grateful that my friends could be with me on this holiday," Kelsey said sweetly. She glanced at Dylan and wondered whether her statement applied to him right now. "Tyler?" she said, calling on him next.

"I'm grateful that Kelsey was kind enough to ask me to join all of you this holiday. It's a pleasure to be with such wonderful people. Dylan?"

"I'm grateful..." he paused, then said, "I'm grateful to have a second chance."

After their afternoon dinner and the football game, Kelsey, Dylan, and Tyler took a walk down to the waterfront. Kelsey and Tyler led the way, and Dylan lagged behind. He seemed to be thinking. Kelsey ignored him, and talked to Tyler, who it seemed, had decided to ignore Dylan's moodiness as well.

"Did you like dinner?"

"It was really good," Tyler said.

"Not as good as Margaret," Kelsey said.

"Maybe, but it was nice to not eat alone," Tyler replied.

"You've eaten Thanksgiving alone?" Kelsey said in surprise.

"Only a couple of times," Tyler replied.

"Next time, you'll come home with me," Kelsey said.

"Thank you for inviting me. It's been really nice," Tyler said.

"Despite," Kelsey said, turning back and looking at Dylan.

"Even with," Tyler corrected her.

"I'm glad you could come," Kelsey said. She paused, then asked him, "But instead of having Thanksgiving alone, why don't you have Thanksgiving with Ryan or Zach?"

"Zach's uncle usually comes to visit, or the Paynes go to his house. He's awful. I met him once, and I hope not to see him again," Tyler said.

"Why?"

"He hasn't gotten over the fact that his brother married someone Japanese. I don't know how Zach tolerates it," Tyler said.

"What about Ryan?"

"Ryan used to go to his Mom's house every other Thanksgiving, then every Thanksgiving, then he started skipping Thanksgiving altogether, and going to out to party."

"Bob doesn't have Thanksgiving?" Kelsey asked.

"I think the holidays bring up bad memories for him. He works straight through them, just like my mom," Tyler said.

"I see. Well, you're always welcome at my house," Kelsey said.

"Thank you," Tyler said. He glanced at Dylan. "Is he okay?"

"He will be," Kelsey said. "He's got some stuff to work out."

"It's the perfect place for it. It's so peaceful here," Tyler said.

"Medina's quiet," Kelsey said.

"Medina's boring," Tyler replied. "There are things to do here. Like go on a walk with my Kelsey."

"Your Kelsey?"

"Exactly," Tyler replied. "Aren't you?"

"Stop being complicated, Tyler. I have to deal with Dylan this weekend," Kelsey said.

"Okay. I'll annoy you again when we get back to Darrow," Tyler replied.

"Thanks," Kelsey said. "Dylan?" she called.

"Yeah," Dylan replied.

"Are you okay back there?" Kelsey asked.

"I'm fine," Dylan said.

"I'm sure," Kelsey said under her breath. "I'm going to text Morgan and have her meet us, okay?" she called back to him.

"Okay," Dylan replied.

Kelsey pulled out her phone and sent a message. She received a reply almost immediately.

"She's on the way," Kelsey said to Tyler, putting the phone in her pocket. "She'll meet us downtown, in front of the store."

"Does she live far away?" Tyler asked.

Kelsey shook her head. "Not really, but she'll drive. If she drives Morgan speed, she'll beat us there." They walked by the athletic field and crossed the street. Dylan was almost a half block behind.

"Let's wait," Kelsey said, a little impatiently. She and Tyler stopped, and Dylan arrived a few moments later. She and Tyler began to walk again. They walked down the block and turned down Water Street. Tyler looked around in interest at all of the Victorian buildings.

"It's like stepping back in time," he commented.

"A little. Except everywhere has wifi," Kelsey said. "And you can order a latte."

"Stop ruining my fantasy," Tyler said.

"Sorry," Kelsey said, giggling.

They walked down the deserted street to the North Wilderness Store, which sparkled with Christmas lights. Morgan was standing outside, wrapped in a long coat.

"Hey, babe," she said.

"Hey," Kelsey replied. "How's it going?"

"You can imagine," Morgan commented.

"I can. That's why I messaged you."

"You're an angel," Morgan said. "What are we doing?"

"Walking around," Kelsey said.

"Sounds good," Morgan said. "Hi, guys," she said to Tyler and Dylan.

"Hi," Tyler said. Dylan didn't speak.

Morgan raised her eyebrows, but Kelsey shook her head.

"Don't ask," she whispered.

"I won't," Morgan said, taking Kelsey's arm. "How was dinner?"

"The usual," Kelsey said.

"So what do you think of our little town?" Morgan asked Tyler, her highlighted brown hair blowing in the cool breeze off the water.

"I love it," Tyler said.

"Really?" Morgan said, glancing at Kelsey.

"So I hear," Kelsey replied.

"You should get out more," Morgan said to him. Tyler laughed.

"How's Jazz?" Kelsey asked Morgan.

"Unreachable. I bet she turned off her phone," Morgan replied.

"Well, she is at Jim's grandmother's," Kelsey said.

"Poor thing," Morgan said.

"What's wrong with being there?" Tyler asked curiously.

"Jim's grandmother is fine, but she lives in the middle of nowhere, and Jazz is stuck out there until tomorrow," Morgan said.

"She'll live," Kelsey said. "One of the hazards of marrying Jim."

"One of," Morgan editorialized.

"He really isn't that bad," Kelsey said. "And he really cares for her."

"I guess," Morgan said.

Kelsey laughed. She looked back at Dylan, who had fallen behind again.

"Come on, Shaw," she said. "Catch up."

"Coming," Dylan said dully.

"Where are we going?" Morgan asked.

"Let's walk the long way back to my house," Kelsey said. "We can eat cookies. My mother baked about a thousand of them. I'll drive you to your car later."

"Sounds like a plan," Morgan said. They turned and began to head back toward Kelsey's, Tyler directly behind them, Dylan still further behind.

"Tyler, where do you live?" Morgan asked.

"Medina," Tyler replied.

"Where's that? she asked.

"On Lake Washington. Across from Seattle," Tyler replied.

"Do you have a big house?"

"Very," Kelsey replied. "It's the size of downtown."

"It is not. It's quite modest for Medina," Tyler said.

"You're kidding," Kelsey said.

"Kelsey, Bill Gates lives in Medina. Trust me, our house is like a shack," Tyler said.

"Nice shack," Kelsey said.

"I like your house better," Tyler said.

"That's because you haven't had to live there," Kelsey replied.

"What is your house like?" Morgan asked, fascinated.

"Tell her, Kelsey," Tyler said.

"You've been inside?" Morgan said.

"Yes."

"You tell us nothing," Morgan pouted.

"It's nice, Morgan. Lots of art," Kelsey said. "Beautiful views of the lake."

"It sounds great," Morgan said dreamily.

"It's boring," Tyler said.

"Please. There's a pool outside," Kelsey said.

"No way," Morgan said.

"You should see Ryan's house, Morgan," Tyler said. "He has two pools, inside and out."

"Really?" Morgan said.

"They have a screening room too. It's like a giant playhouse," Tyler commented.

"I'm so jealous," Morgan said.

"Don't be," Tyler said. "I'd rather be here."

"Of course you would, Kelsey's here," Dylan commented. Tyler and the girls looked back at him.

"You're right. What's a house without people?" Tyler said.

"Poor little rich boy," Dylan said.

"You're not exactly poor yourself, Mr. Shaw," Tyler replied. "So lay off."

"Whatever," Dylan said, lapsing back into silence.

Morgan glanced at Kelsey, who shrugged her shoulders.

"Do you travel a lot?" Morgan asked Tyler.

"Not really," Tyler said.

"His Mom's in Asia right now," Kelsey said.

"Really? Wow. I loved your pictures from New York. I'd give anything to go," Morgan said to Kelsey.

"You went to New York?" Dylan asked Kelsey.

"Spring break," Kelsey said.

"With Jess?" Dylan asked.

"Tyler too, right?" Morgan said, then she bit her lip.

"Yes, Morgan," Kelsey said, giving her a look.

Sorry. Morgan mouthed.

Kelsey hugged her arm.

"You went to New York with Tyler?" Dylan said. "She went with you?"

"I stayed with Jess," Kelsey said.

"You're really unbelievable," Dylan said.

"What?" Kelsey said.

"Dylan, what's the big deal?" Tyler said.

"You've just taken over her life, haven't you?" Dylan said.

"Hardly," Tyler commented.

"What's next, living together?" Dylan said.

"Would that bother you?" Tyler asked him.

"Yeah, it would. I've only been gone a year," Dylan said.

"And she was supposed to wait for you?" Tyler asked.

Dylan frowned. "She wasn't supposed to get involved with you," he said.

"It's her life," Tyler said.

"She's not for sale," Dylan replied.

"Dylan, stop it. Really, this is ridiculous," Kelsey said.

"Yeah, you're right, it is. What's wrong with you?" Dylan said.

"What's wrong with me? What's wrong with you? Tyler and I are friends, so get over it," Kelsey said.

"You couldn't stand him when I was there," Dylan snapped. "What did he do, buy you a car?"

"That does it," Kelsey seethed. She stopped on the street corner and turned to him. "I'll tell you what he did. When I was a wreck after you left, Tyler was there for me. When I was stressed out about exams, he studied with me. When my summer roommate was crazy, he offered me a place to stay. Where were you?" she snapped.

Dylan glared at her. "You know where I was," he said.

"I understand that you needed to take care of yourself. But maybe I needed someone to take care of me too," Kelsey said. "I'm not going to apologize for that."

"I'm not asking you to," Dylan said. "I just can't believe how quickly you changed your tune about him."

"Believe it," Kelsey said sharply.

Dylan glared at Tyler. "Maybe I should go," Dylan said.

"That's your decision. I want you to stay, but I want you to stop blaming Tyler because you weren't there for me. That's on you," Kelsey said.

"I wanted to be," Dylan said quietly.

"I know. And I wanted you to be. But you weren't. And Tyler was," Kelsey said.

"Fine," Dylan said. He sighed deeply. "Fine." He began walking again and the other three followed him. Morgan gave Kelsey's shoulders a hug.

"Good job, North. You tell 'em," Morgan said in her ear.

The group walked in silence back to Kelsey's house. Kelsey opened the door and Dylan headed up the stairs.

"I'm going to bed."

Morgan looked at him. "It's not even eight," she said.

"I'm tired," Dylan said, and he left.

"Whatever. Let's get cookies," Kelsey said, leading them into the kitchen.

Mrs. North looked up. She had been reading on the kitchen counter. "Hi, Morgan," she said.

"Hi, Kelly," Morgan said.

"Where's Dylan?" Mrs. North asked Kelsey.

"Upstairs," Kelsey said, retrieving a plate of cookies.

"Is it cold out?" Mrs. North asked.

"A little. Is Dad still watching football?"

"Yes, but he's in our room. He needed to lie down after eating."

"I'm not surprised," Kelsey said.

"It was really great, Mrs. North," Tyler said.

"I'm glad you enjoyed it, Tyler," Mrs. North said.

"Let's go downstairs," Kelsey said, taking the plate of cookies and leading them to the basement.

They walked downstairs and settled themselves into the chairs in front of the television. Kelsey passed Tyler the plate of cookies after taking one for herself.

"So what's Dylan's problem?" Morgan asked, as Tyler passed her the plate of cookies.

"Who knows?" Kelsey said. "I don't care. I didn't invite him."

"I can't believe your Mom did that to you," Morgan laughed, taking a bite of her cookie.

"I have a feeling your Mom and mine could trade notes," Tyler said.

"I never thought about that. Yeah, my Mom's pretty tricky," Kelsey said. "Too bad she didn't use it to make us billions of dollars."

"She makes great cookies though," Tyler said.

"Yeah, that makes up for the billions," Kelsey teased.

"Let's play a game," Morgan said.

"As long as it's not truth or dare," Tyler said, biting his cookie.

Kelsey laughed loudly. "You're not so good at that," she said.

"Tell me about it," Tyler agreed.

"No, not that. I want to know the most crazy things you've seen rich people do."

"That's not a game," Kelsey said.

"It's fun. You can play too. I bet you've seen stuff now, especially since you went to New York."

"Like Ryan taking Kim to London?" Tyler said to Kelsey.

"On a date," Kelsey said to Morgan. "For one night."

"No way," Morgan said.

"Really, we could just list the things Ryan did between the ages of 16 and now, and we probably would cover everything," Tyler said.

"He really has a reputation," Kelsey said. "Okay, that party was pretty crazy," she said. "Morgan, in New York, there must have been a thousand people. They rented a building, had three DJs, and free everything."

"Incredible," Morgan said.

"Bob's third wife spent a quarter of a million dollars on a ring," Tyler said.

"She didn't," Kelsey said.

"She did. Bob made her take it back," Tyler said.

"How you take something like that back? Do they ask for the receipt?" Morgan asked.

Kelsey giggled.

"Does your mom have a plane?" Morgan asked.

"The company does," Tyler said. "So does Ryan's father."

"Bob has a plane?" Kelsey asked.

"Yeah, he's thinking about buying a larger one. The one he has can't fly across the country without being refueled," Tyler said.

"Okay, that's crazy. Your own plane," Morgan said.

"What's crazier is he mostly uses it to take women to dinner," Tyler said.

"What?" Kelsey said.

"Los Angeles, Las Vegas. It's insane," Tyler said. "This why Ryan thinks his lifestyle is normal."

"I can't even imagine that," Morgan said.

"You have to think bigger," Tyler said.

"Does your mother spend like Ryan's father?" Morgan asked.

"Never. The most expensive thing my mother has bought is her house. Although she does spend a lot on litigation, particularly with Chris."

"Tyler's father," Kelsey explained to Morgan. "She wears fabulous jewelry. Does Bob buy all of it?" Kelsey asked.

"I think so. The only thing my mother really shops for is acquisitions," Tyler said.

"Does Jeffrey pick out her clothes?" Kelsey asked.

"I'll tell you a secret," Tyler said. "But you can't tell anyone but Jess."

"Really? Okay," Kelsey said.

"My mother isn't a morning person. And a lot of nights, she stays up late watching the fashion channel. When she sees a designer she likes, sometimes she'll buy the entire collection."

"Lisa Olsen is into fashion?" Kelsey said.

"What would Wall Street say?" Tyler joked.

"Her clothes are beautiful," Kelsey said to Morgan. "She wears a lot of silk."

"It sounds like a dream," Morgan said.

"She works a lot," Kelsey said. "I bet that makes it less fun."

"My mother would say that her work is fun," Tyler said to Kelsey.

"I guess she would," Kelsey said. "I want to be able to say that too."

"You enjoyed your summer. Maybe you'll be able to, once you're a lawyer," Tyler said.

"I hope so," Kelsey said.

"Kelsey, did you ever re-wear that dress from last Christmas?" Morgan asked.

"It's sitting in the closet. Along with everything else Tyler's bought," Kelsey said, looking at him.

"We don't go out enough for you to wear the same thing twice," Tyler said. "Save them, one day we will."

"Oh, will we?"

"Yes, we will, Miss North," Tyler said.

"I told you to stop being complicated and I meant it," Kelsey said.

"Sorry," Tyler said. He took another cookie.

The trio stayed up, watched TV, and ate cookies until 11 p.m. when Morgan said she needed to head back.

"Do you want me to drive you?" Tyler asked her.

"It's okay, Kelsey can give me a ride back to my car," Morgan said yawning.

"Are you sure?" Tyler asked.

"It's fine, Tyler. It's pretty safe here," Kelsey said.

"Everyone knows everything," Morgan added.

"Okay. I'll stay up for you," Tyler said.

"You don't have to," Kelsey said.

"Of course I do," Tyler said. "Be safe and hurry back."

"All right," Kelsey said. She and Morgan got their coats and climbed the stairs. Kelsey took the keys for the pickup truck off of a hook by the door.

"Morgan, take some cookies home," Kelsey said. "My mom left some for you."

"Okay. Thanks," Morgan said. Kelsey picked up a plastic container containing cookies which had a post-it note that said, *Morgan*, and handed it to her. Then they walked out into the cold.

The girls jumped into the pickup truck and Kelsey started it up and flipped on the heat.

"It's going to be cold this winter," Morgan said, wrapping her coat tightly around herself.

"I know," Kelsey said. "I should steal some of my mom's sweaters."

"So what's your deal with Tyler?" Morgan asked as they drove off.

"What do you mean?"

"Don't play dumb, Kels. I know you like him," Morgan said.

"I do," Kelsey said.

"And?"

"And nothing. Tyler hasn't asked me out."

"So ask him out."

"No," Kelsey said.

"Why not?" Morgan asked.

"He's not ready."

"Ready for a date?"

"Ready to date me," Kelsey corrected.

"Why?"

"His friends say it's because he's serious about me, but I have my doubts," Kelsey said as they headed down the hill.

"What do you think?" Morgan asked.

"I don't know what to think," Kelsey said.

"What do you think about Dylan?" Morgan asked. "He was really weird tonight."

"He certainly was. I don't know what to think about him either. I think I won't think about either of them and just eat all weekend," Kelsey said as she turned down Water Street.

"You live an interesting life," Morgan said. "Surrounded by rich guys, living in the city, traveling around the country."

"I guess. Some days I wish I was back here."

"You do not," Morgan said.

"I do. It's home," Kelsey said.

"I'll trade you anytime," Morgan said.

"I'll let you know," Kelsey said. She pulled next to Morgan's car, which was sitting alone in the North Wilderness Store parking lot. "Message me when you get home," she said.

"I will. Tell your mom thanks for the cookies," Morgan said, getting out of the truck.

"Okay," Kelsey replied. Morgan shut the door and waved. She got into her own car, and both girls drove off.

Kelsey returned home, and as she expected, Tyler was waiting for her. He had put the extra cookies away and washed the dishes that were left in the kitchen. He was drying his hands when Kelsey walked in.

"Everything okay?" Tyler asked.

"Yes, thanks," Kelsey said. She leaned against the counter and looked at him. Tyler looked back at her.

"Miss North? You have something to say?" he said.

Kelsey sighed. "I'm sorry Dylan is giving you such a hard time."

"Dylan's fine," Tyler said. "But are you?"

"I'm feeling bad. I invited you," Kelsey said.

"You didn't ask Dylan to come. I'd rather be here with you and deal with him, than be in Medina watching television," Tyler said.

"Are you sure?" Kelsey asked.

"Absolutely," Tyler replied. "Anyway, I understand where he's coming from. He thought he was going to have you all to himself this weekend and that's not going to happen."

Kelsey smiled.

"Is that what you had thought? That you would have me all to yourself this weekend?" she teased.

"I didn't say that. I'm not allowed to be complicated," Tyler replied.

"No, you aren't," Kelsey said. Her phone beeped with a message, and she glanced at it. "Morgan's home," she said.

"Good. I was going to ask," Tyler said.

"Do you want to go to bed?" Kelsey asked. She was getting tired.

"Do you think Dylan's asleep?" Tyler asked.

"Why?"

"I really don't want to get yelled at again tonight," Tyler replied.

"What was he yelling about before dinner?"

"The same thing he's been complaining about since we got here. The fact that I've had the audacity to speak to you over the past year."

"Dylan's insane," Kelsey said. "I really don't understand why he's got it out for you this weekend."

"He's on a mission, and my presence is ruining it."

"I'm the one who's ruined it. I'm not interested in him," Kelsey said.

"He's never going to accept that," Tyler said. "I wouldn't."

Kelsey looked at him. "Well, that's because you know it's not true."

"Who's being complicated now, Miss North?" Tyler smiled.

"Not me," Kelsey said.

"Hmm," Tyler replied. "I'm going to bed now."

"That's probably for the best," Kelsey replied. "Good night, Tyler."

"Good night," Tyler said, and he left the kitchen.

The next morning, Kelsey woke up early and walked down the hall to the bathroom. As she passed by her own room, she could hear talking.

Unlike the day before, it seemed civil. She still heard talking when she passed by again, and headed downstairs.

Her parents were in the kitchen, her mother by the stove and her father standing drinking coffee at the counter.

"Morning, Kels," her father said.

"Hi," Kelsey said.

"No run today?" her mother asked.

"We were up late with Morgan," Kelsey said, looking in the fridge for juice.

"How is she?" Kelsey's father asked.

"Okay," Kelsey said, having located the juice. She put it on the counter and got a glass.

"Really?" her father asked.

"Dad, you know how things are over there," Kelsey said, pouring the cranberry juice into the glass.

"I know," her father replied.

"Let Morgan know if she needs anything, to let us know," her mother said.

"I will," Kelsey said.

"Will you see her today?" her father asked.

"Morgan's working today. She wants the overtime," Kelsey replied.

"At least she's got a good job," her mother said.

"She loves it. Keeps her out of the house," Kelsey said.

"I really wish Walt would accept some help, so everything didn't fall on Morgan's shoulders," Mrs. North said.

"Walter Hill will never admit that he needs anything from anybody," Mr. North said.

"It's a shame," Mrs. North concluded. "So what are you kids doing today?"

"Jazz is coming over and we're going to Silverdale," Kelsey said, drinking her juice.

"Are you taking Dylan and Tyler?" her mother asked.

"If they want to go," Kelsey said. "I'm sure Tyler will. I don't know about Dylan."

"What do you mean?" her mother asked.

"Dylan's in a bad mood," Kelsey said to her.

"I haven't noticed that," her mother said.

"You haven't been around him," Kelsey replied. She glanced at her father, who gave her a sympathetic smile.

"I see," Mrs. North said.

"How's Tyler liking PT?" Mr. North asked.

"He says he likes it a lot," Kelsey said, as she finished her juice.

"I'm surprised," Mrs. North said. "I imagine it would be too boring for someone like him."

"Someone like him?" Kelsey asked sweetly.

Her mother shrugged. "Well, he's very cosmopolitan, isn't he?" her mother said.

"He seems pretty down to earth to me," Kelsey's father said.

His wife glared at him. "Oh, come on Dan. He went to Harvard," Kelsey's mother commented.

"Kelsey goes to Darrow," her father countered. "She's not a snob."

"Oh, but I am, Dad," Kelsey teased. "I'm very particular about who I want to spend my time with."

Her father laughed and her mother frowned.

"What does that mean, Kelsey Anne North?" her mother asked.

"Next time, perhaps, you'll let me decide who to invite home for the holidays," Kelsey replied quietly.

"It's my house too," her mother replied.

"Then you should entertain your guest," Kelsey replied.

"Kels," her father scolded.

"I should have been warned," Kelsey said.

"It never occurred to me that it would be a problem," Mrs. North said.

"It wouldn't be, if Dylan wasn't being a jerk," Kelsey said softly.

"Why are you blaming Dylan?" her mother asked.

Kelsey sighed. "Next time, warn me," she said.

"I'm your mother."

"I know that, but this isn't a relaxing vacation for me," Kelsey said.

Mr. North looked at his wife. "Kelsey has a point. She wasn't expecting to have to entertain two people."

"I wasn't expecting her to either," her mother commented.

Kelsey took a piece of toast, and bit into it. She and her parents stood in the kitchen silently. A few minutes, they heard footsteps on the stairs and Tyler walked in, fully dressed in jeans and a Darrow Law sweatshirt.

"Good morning," he said, looking around.

"Hi, Tyler," Kelsey said.

"Good morning," her mother said, with an affected tone.

"Good morning, Tyler," her father said, giving his wife a look.

"Dylan will be down in a minute," he said.

"Do you want some breakfast?" Kelsey asked.

"Sure," Tyler said. "Can I help?"

"It's fine," Mrs. North said.

"I'll get you some juice," Kelsey said, going back into the fridge for the orange juice.

"Thanks," Tyler said.

"I'll bring it to the dining room," Kelsey offered.

"Okay," Tyler said, taking the hint and leaving the kitchen.

She glared at her mother, who ignored her.

"Tyler's my guest," she said softly.

"I'm well aware of that, Kelsey," her mother snapped.

"Maybe I'll stay in Seattle for Christmas," Kelsey commented.

"Is that a threat?" her mother asked sharply.

"Never mind," Kelsey said, taking the juice and a glass into the dining room.

Tyler looked up when she walked in.

"I could go back to Medina. I have plenty to do," he said.

"Shut up, Olsen. This is my problem. I'll deal with it," Kelsey said, setting the glass in front of him.

"Yes, Ma'am," Tyler said, taking the juice from her.

Kelsey sat next to him as he poured orange juice into his glass.

"I don't have to ask if your mother would do this to you, because I know she does it all of the time," she said.

"Nothing like a good ambush," Tyler said. "Throws the enemy off."

"Is your own child the enemy?"

"In my mother's world, everyone is the enemy," Tyler said, taking a sip of his drink. "It's like ancient times. Trust no one."

"I guess that simplifies things," Kelsey commented. "Want to go to the mall?"

"There's a mall here?"

"About an hour away," Kelsey replied.

"Sure," Tyler smiled at her. "I am actually having fun, Kels."

Kelsey shook her head. "I'm not sure how that's possible," she replied.

Dylan came down about ten minutes later, and Mrs. North seemed cheerier. As a matter of fact, so did Dylan, to Kelsey's surprise. They all ate breakfast, and Jasmine arrived about an hour after the breakfast dishes were done. Dylan offered to drive them to Silverdale and they all piled into his BMW, Jasmine and Kelsey in the back seat.

Jasmine was her usual upbeat self as she talked with Kelsey about the places she wanted to go in the mall, and what she was looking to buy. In the meantime, Dylan drove while Tyler silently looked out of the window.

Dylan parked the car, and they got out.

"Where first?" Jasmine asked Kelsey.

"The bookstore would be great, I'd like to look at the IP books."

"IP?" Jasmine asked.

"Intellectual property. The kind of law I'm studying this semester," Kelsey explained.

"What are you studying now, Tyler?" Dylan asked him as they entered the mall.

"IP as well."

"You just can't leave her alone," Dylan said. Kelsey looked back at him.

"Tyler's the one who gave me the idea. His mother was an IP lawyer,"

Kelsey said.

"Before she became a mogul?" Dylan asked sarcastically.

"Why, yes, that's right," Tyler replied.

"Don't you get tired of living in her shadow?" Dylan said.

"I do. That's why I'm at Darrow," Tyler said.

"I heard you she's planning on making you CEO," Dylan said.

"I've heard that too," Tyler said unhappily.

"Dylan, drop it," Kelsey said as they entered the bookstore. Tyler and Jasmine stopped by the newsstand, while Kelsey and Dylan continued into the heart of the store. Kelsey looked around for the legal section.

"He's so fake," Dylan said.

Kelsey scowled. "What?"

"'I don't want to be CEO. I don't care about the money.' Get real," Dylan said.

"Dylan, you don't even know him," Kelsey said.

"Of course I do. I roomed with his stupid friend. All Matthew talked about was money."

"Matthew failed out. Anyway, Tyler isn't really friends with him."

"He failed out? Good, he was an idiot."

"You're just a bundle of fun," Kelsey commented, finding the legal section and looking at the books.

"What does that mean?" Dylan said sharply.

"It means you're really being a pain," Kelsey said.

"Why are you defending him?"

"Tyler? Because he's perfectly decent," Kelsey said. "I don't know what your problem is today."

"My problem? I don't have a problem," Dylan said.

"Clearly you do," Kelsey said. She looked up. Tyler and Jasmine were walking toward them.

"Fine, spend your time with him. If you don't want me here, I'm going back to Portland," Dylan snapped at Kelsey, and he walked off.

"Good going, North. You blew our ride," Jasmine teased her as she and Tyler walked up.

"Whatever," Kelsey said. She was completely sick of Dylan. Tyler glanced at Kelsey, smiled, and shook his head. He pulled out his phone and sent a message as they continued walking through the bookstore. Dylan was nowhere to be seen.

After Dylan left, things improved dramatically for Kelsey. She joined Tyler and Jasmine, who was in a quest for a pair of jeans that fit her petite frame. She finally found them at the Gap.

After Jasmine bought two pairs and nagged Kelsey into buying a v-neck sweater that Kelsey had to admit was very flattering, they had lunch at a restaurant in the mall. Per usual, Tyler had insisted on paying.

Lunch over, and a bit more shopping later, Kelsey was ready to go. She had spent most of the money she had brought on the sweater, and even Jasmine seemed shopped out.

"So are you ready to head back?" Kelsey asked her.

"Sure. What do you want to do? Wait until Morgan gets off and have her pick us up?" Jasmine asked her.

"That or I can call my Dad. Our store's not closing until seven, though," Kelsey said thoughtfully.

"We can go when you want. Martin's waiting for us," Tyler said.

"Martin?" Kelsey asked in surprise.

"Dylan Shaw isn't going to dictate my schedule," Tyler said.

"Who's Martin?" Jasmine asked.

"Tyler's driver," Kelsey said. "Martin's here? In Silverdale?"

"He is," Tyler replied.

"Then let's go," Jasmine said.

"Okay," Kelsey said.

Tyler looked at his phone. "He's parked outside JC Penney."

"I know where that is," Jasmine said brightly. She led them through the mall, through JC Penney and out to the parking lot. A limousine sat by the sidewalk, and Martin got out of the driver's seat when he saw the trio.

"Good afternoon, Sir," Martin said to Tyler as they walked up. Kelsey noticed that he seemed a bit amused.

"Hi, Martin," Tyler said.

"Miss North," Martin said in greeting to Kelsey as he opened the door for them.

"Hi, Martin," she replied, as she got into the car.

"This is Miss Jefferson," Tyler said to him.

"Miss Jefferson," Martin said.

"Hi," Jasmine said brightly. She followed Kelsey into the car, bags in hand, and Tyler followed with the rest of her bags. On the seat there was a flat wicker basket full of baked goods with a folded note. Kelsey glanced at the note as they strapped themselves in. She realized that it wasn't in English.

"Language?" she asked Tyler. He looked at the basket.

"Norwegian. It says have a nice weekend." Tyler took the note off the basket, unfolded it and read the inside.

"You speak Norwegian?" Kelsey asked him.

"I wouldn't say speak. I can greet my grandmother, swear, and ask Margaret for things."

"Swear?" Kelsey asked.

"Margaret has a mouth like a sailor. My grandmother is scandalized when she comes to visit," Tyler replied. He placed the note back in the basket.

"You're Norwegian?" Jasmine asked.

"Among other things," Tyler replied. He took the cover off of the basket. "Want one?" he asked.

"Sure," Kelsey said. Tyler handed each of them M&M brownies and took one for himself.

"Miss North, where should I drop the three of you?" Martin asked her, as they drove out of the mall parking lot.

"Outside of town?" Kelsey asked Jasmine. "Do you want to explain the limo to your Dad?"

"Not really, but I don't want to walk either. Let's get dropped off at your house. Hopefully your neighbors aren't home yet," Jasmine said.

"My house please, Martin," Kelsey said.

"Very good," Martin replied to her.

"So do you think Dylan went back to Portland? Or will he be sitting at your house ready for round three?" Tyler asked Kelsey.

"Do not mention Dylan Shaw to me," Kelsey warned him. Tyler grinned.

"He's really weird this vacation. Actually, he always seems weird to me," Jasmine said.

"Yeah, you haven't seen any other side of Dylan," Kelsey said thoughtfully.

"Maybe Thanksgiving doesn't bring out the best in him," Jasmine said. "Tyler, these are great brownies," she said, taking another bite.

"How did Margaret have time to send brownies to you?" Kelsey asked.

"Martin was running an errand for Jeffrey when I requested that he pick us up. I imagine she made them while he was finishing. There was no hurry," Tyler said. Kelsey nodded. Once again, Tyler's forethought had saved the day. Medina was at least an hour and a half away from the mall.

Kelsey ate her brownie and looked out of the window as they headed up Route 3. She wasn't sure if she wanted Dylan to be at her house or not. Tyler was right, if Dylan was there, he'd keep fighting with her, but if he wasn't, she was concerned that it might be the end of their friendship. And despite this holiday, Kelsey didn't know how she felt about that.

Kelsey and Dylan had been so close during college. They had bonded instantly, and she thought of him as one of her dearest friends. But the past few days had made Kelsey wonder if things had permanently changed for the worst.

She glanced at Tyler and Jasmine, who were discussing yesterday's Seahawks game. Jasmine was a huge sports fan. This was what she had been expecting, peace and quiet with the people that she loved and cared for. Instead she felt like she was in the middle of a constant fire fight. And what was particularly frustrating for her, was that she still couldn't wrap her mind around the fact that Dylan was angry about her friendship with Tyler.

Despite what Dylan had said, Kelsey didn't believe that Dylan was really in love with her. And she didn't believe that Dylan was upset about Tyler's new wealth or any of the reasons he had complained about him over the past few days. Dylan was going through some internal struggle, Kelsey was sure, but he was taking it out on everyone else. She sighed and took another brownie.

They drove the hour back to Port Townsend, Tyler and Jasmine talking, and Kelsey looking out of the window. Every so often during the trip, Jasmine would pat Kelsey's arm sympathetically, or Kelsey would catch Tyler looking at her in concern, but neither of them interrupted her reverie. Martin pulled up to Kelsey's house. No BMW sat outside.

Tyler helped Jasmine walk her bags back to her house, while Kelsey paced in her living room and debated whether to call Dylan. Finally she decided to let it go. If Dylan wanted to come back, he would. If not, Kelsey would move on. It was his choice.

Earlier than expected, Kelsey heard the front door open. She glanced up expecting to see Tyler. Dylan stood at the door.

"Dylan," Kelsey said to him. Dylan walked over with her with determination, took her into his arms and before she could react, kissed her on the lips. Kelsey slapped him.

Dylan broke away from her in surprise.

"What are you doing?" Kelsey shouted.

Dylan rubbed his face where she had hit him. He stepped closer to her.

"Don't even think it," Kelsey warned him.

Dylan looked into her eyes. "Why? Because you're in love with Tyler?" he challenged her.

"Yes," Kelsey replied.

Dylan's face fell. "What?"

"I'm in love with Tyler. Not you," Kelsey said.

"Does he know?"

"Probably," Kelsey said.

"He doesn't seem to care," Dylan said. "He's not going out with you."

Kelsey felt the pierce to her heart, but she ignored it.

"This isn't about him," she said.

"Why are you doing this, Kelsey? Why are you leaving me behind?" Dylan said.

Kelsey looked at Dylan in dismay. Then she took a deep breath. He was right.

"Because I won't be dragged back," Kelsey said bravely. "I've been where you are. I won't go back, no matter how much I care for you. I'm going to keep going forward."

"He'll never accept you. You know that, right? He'll never be yours," Dylan said.

Kelsey closed her eyes.

"I want you," Dylan continued. "Why don't you see that?"

Kelsey opened her eyes and looked at him. "You want yourself back. The old Dylan, the one you were before you went to Darrow. But I can't give that back to you. Only you can," Kelsey said.

"Why don't you understand me?" Dylan asked her.

"I understand you too well, Dylan. If you focus on me, on Tyler, you don't have to work on yourself. I'm not going to let you do that."

"Who are you, my counselor?"

"No, I'm your friend. And no matter how angry you make me, you will always be my friend, Dylan," Kelsey felt herself tear up. "I'm sorry this is so hard for you. I really am," she said.

Dylan sat on the arm of a chair. He sighed.

"You have no idea," he whispered. Kelsey walked over to him and put her arm around his shoulder. Dylan looked up at her. "I'm sorry. I should go home."

The front door opened. Tyler walked in, saw them, and walked back out.

"What do I do?" Dylan asked her, ignoring the interruption. "Tell me what to do."

Kelsey sighed. "Stop fighting."

"You?"

"Yourself," Kelsey replied.

"I can't accept what happened to me," Dylan said, shaking his head.

"You have no choice," Kelsey replied.

"If I accept it, I have to accept it all. I have to admit that I lost control of my life," Dylan said.

"You did," Kelsey said. "But it doesn't mean that you don't have control now. Dylan, every day you can make things better."

"Like you."

"Like me," Kelsey said.

Dylan looked up at her. "I've always admired you Kels. But I don't know if I can do what you did."

"Of course you can. I'm no better than you," Kelsey said. "Neither is Tyler," she added. "He has flaws too."

"Golden boy? No way," Dylan said.

"You'd be surprised," Kelsey replied.

"Really?"

Kelsey nodded.

"Want to share?"

Kelsey laughed. "No. Just trust me."

"I will," Dylan sighed again. "I'm really sorry. I've ruined your break."

"It's okay," Kelsey said. "However, you can stop now."

Dylan looked at Kelsey. Finally he shook his head and laughed. "I'll try."

"Try hard," Kelsey said, smiling at him.

"I should apologize to Jasmine. How did you get back home?" Dylan said, standing.

"You don't want to know," Kelsey replied.

"Tyler has a helicopter?" Dylan guessed.

"Limo," Kelsey answered.

"Of course," Dylan said.

Kelsey giggled. "I said you didn't want to know," she replied.

"Is it still okay if I despise him?" Dylan said.

"Yes. But stop yelling at him."

"I will," Dylan said.

"Want a brownie?" Kelsey asked.

"Did Tyler make them?" Dylan asked.

"His chef," Kelsey laughed.

Dylan sighed. "I really do despise him," he said. "Where are they?"

Kelsey took Dylan to the kitchen and set him up with a plate of brownies and a glass of milk. Then she wandered out to the backyard shed. Tyler was inside, cleaning up.

"Hey," she said.

"Everything okay?" he asked in concern.

"For now," Kelsey said.

"Jasmine sent that over," Tyler said, gesturing to a paper bag on the counter.

Kelsey looked inside and laughed. She pulled out one of the numerous teddy bears that commonly sat on Jasmine's bed. When Kelsey had lived at the Jefferson house, and on every one of her overnight visits since, Jasmine had given Kelsey one of the bears. "In case you need some comfort," Jazz always said.

Tyler looked up at her quizzically.

"It's a loaner," Kelsey said, hugging it.

For the rest of the day, Dylan tried to make amends. He walked over and apologized to Jasmine, he stopped complaining to Kelsey, and he even kept his rude comments about Tyler to a minimum when they went to dinner with her parents that evening.

"So boys, do you want to hear the story of how I met Kelsey's mom?" Mr. North asked as they were eating.

"Oh, Dan, it's so boring," Mrs. North said.

"It is not, is it Kels?"

"It's scary. It reminds me of how close I came to not existing," Kelsey

commented.

Tyler looked at her. "Really?" he asked her. Kelsey nodded.

"Now I've got to tell it," Mr. North said to Mrs. North.

"Fine," she said.

"So Kelly and I are both from Sequim."

"Where the lavender festival is," Kelsey commented to Tyler.

"Right," Mr. North said, continuing. "We were high school sweethearts."

"Not for long," Kelsey commented.

"Is this your story or mine, Miss Kelsey?" Mr. North admonished her.

"Technically both," Kelsey said.

"Anyway," Mr. North continued, giving Kelsey a look. "I went to the UW in Seattle, and Kelly moved to Port Townsend to get her degree. We decided to take a break from dating for a while, but we stayed in touch."

Kelsey glanced at Tyler, who seemed interested in the story. Dylan, on the other hand, dragged his fork through his potatoes.

"So I finished the UW and stayed in Seattle, while Kelly had moved back home to Sequim. One Christmas I came home, and as I usually did, I dropped by Kelly's parents' house."

"I had skipped going home for Thanksgiving that year, so it had been a while since I had seen Kelly."

"Too long," Kelsey editorialized.

"Exactly," Mr. North said, without missing a beat. "So when I walked in, I asked Kelly's mom where she was. 'Out with Greg,' was her answer."

"Who's Greg?" Tyler asked.

"That's what I said. I had no idea who Greg was either. So I sat right down on the couch and I waited for Kelly to return home," Mr. North said.

Kelsey smiled. This was one of her favorite parts of the story.

"And I waited. And waited and waited. I got there at two in the afternoon and Kelly didn't get back home until after midnight. I ate dinner with her family, sat around and watched TV with her brothers, and watched everyone get up and head for bed, while I continued to sit there waiting for her."

"By the time she walked in, I had worked myself up into quite a state. So when I heard the key in the door, I stood up and said, 'Where have you been, young lady?'"

Kelsey giggled.

"But I wasn't done. I told her how worried I had been, and demanded to know why she had been out so late. And Kelly put her hands on her hips and said, 'Well, Dan, if you had taken me out, you would have known.' Then she walked out of the room and up to bed, without another word."

"I sat back down on that overstuffed couch and stayed there for hours, just thinking. I didn't leave Kelly's house until 3 a.m."

"This is the best part," Kelsey said as an aside to Tyler. He smiled at her, and looked back over at Mr. North.

"So after a few hours of sleep, I headed back over to Kelly's house, just in time for breakfast. I know Kelly's father thought I was crazy, because he told me so later. But Kelly was there, and we had both cooled down a bit. I asked her where she had gone, and she told me she had been Christmas caroling in Brinnon."

"About an hour away," Kelsey said.

"Quiet," Mr. North said to her. Kelsey grinned.

"'With Greg?' I asked her," Mr. North continued. "And she said yes. Kelly's brother Mike asked me to pass the bacon, and as I lifted up the plate, I told Kelly that I didn't want her to date Greg anymore."

"And do you know what Kelly, the love of my life said to me?"

"I do," Kelsey said.

"Of course you do, because you've heard this story a thousand times," Mrs. North said. "Let him tell it for the one thousand and first."

"No. What did she say?" Tyler asked, curiously. Mr. North had paused dramatically.

"Kelly said, 'It's not up to you.'" Mr. North frowned at the memory. "Here we are, at a table surrounded by her family and Kelly's refusing to back down. That was it. I was going to win. So I said, 'Yes, it is up to me. Do you know why it's up to me, Kelly?'"

"Why?" Mrs. North asked, smiling at her husband.

"Because I'm going to marry you," Mr. North responded. Tyler looked at Mr. North in surprise and Kelsey grinned at her dad.

"So Kelsey's mom-to-be not so gently pointed out that I had failed to ask her, and she certainly hadn't agreed."

"This is all going on at the breakfast table?" Tyler asked.

"The whole family is watching us like it's the Super Bowl," Mr. North said. "So I kneel next to Kelly and ask her to marry me, and do you know what she says?"

Tyler shook his head. Dylan looked up as well.

"She asks me where the ring is. Not yes, not no. Where's the ring?"

Tyler and Kelsey laughed.

"You deserved it," Mrs. North said.

"I'm sitting at Kelly's feet, her entire family is looking at me and Kelly wants to know where her ring is. I don't even know what to say," Mr. North said. "So I just sit there, looking up at her."

"Finally, her brother Craig takes pity on me, and he whispers to me, 'Just tell her you'll buy her one.' So that's what I say. And do you know what Kelly says?"

"No," Tyler said. Kelsey glanced at him. He was clearly fascinated by the story.

"She tells me that she's not answering me until I get her a ring. Then she stands up and walks out of the room." Mr. North paused. "So I arrived in Sequim yesterday, I've gotten about five hours of sleep, and Kelly's family is eating breakfast as if my marriage proposal hadn't just been ignored by their only daughter."

"What did you do?" Tyler asked.

Mr. North shrugged. "I sat back down in my chair and finished breakfast," Mr. North commented.

"Daddy," Kelsey said.

"Then," Mr. North said, giving his daughter a smile, "I went back to my house and asked my mother to give me a ring. She asked why, and I said that I was marrying Kelly Parker. My mother looked at me for a good three minutes, then she walked out of the room and returned with a ring. Her own engagement ring. And as I was leaving, she said to me, 'It took you long enough.'"

"So I went back to Kelly's and gave her the ring. And she said yes."

"Only because it was your mother's ring. I didn't want to disappoint her," Mrs. North commented.

Mr. North grinned at his wife. "That was kind of you," he said.

"I thought so," Mrs. North commented.

"Did you ever meet Greg?" Tyler asked.

"I did. A couple of days later. Sequim's a pretty small town, and I ran into him at the 7-11. He introduced himself to me."

"What did he say to you?" Tyler asked.

"Congratulations," Mr. North replied. "Then he told me that he was only two paychecks away from asking Kelly himself. He had been saving up for the ring."

"I might have said no," Mrs. North commented.

"Suppose you had said yes?" Kelsey said. "See, scary," she said to Tyler.

"Lucky for all of us your father asked me first," Mrs. North said.

"Lucky," Tyler said thoughtfully.

After spending Saturday watching making pizza and watching movies with Jasmine, Morgan, and the boys at her house, Kelsey was finally starting to feel relaxed. She was almost looking forward to going back to Darrow, and finding out how Jess and Ryan were doing in New York. She hadn't wanted to disturb them and Jessica hadn't messaged her.

The one thing that still troubled her was Dylan's comments about Tyler never accepting her. She hated to admit it, but it was something she had considered and put tried to put aside. There would always be a part of her that felt like less than worthy of good things, despite her outward confidence. It was the part that had pulled her down before, and a feeling that she fought against daily.

On Sunday morning, Tyler and Dylan were packing their things in her room and Kelsey stood in the kitchen drinking juice. She and Tyler had gone on a run in the morning, just as the sun was peeking over Port Townsend. Even with all of the drama, it had been nice to be home.

"Kels, do you want to take anything back to school?" her mother asked. "I'm packing cookies for Dylan."

"I've eaten too much this vacation, but thanks," Kelsey replied.

"Okay," her mother said. Kelsey glanced at her. She noticed her mother didn't offer to pack anything for Tyler. Kelsey's father walked in and tossed her a package.

"What's this?" Kelsey asked.

"It's a fleece for Tyler. His payment for helping me with the displays."

"I'm sure he doesn't need anything," Kelsey's mother commented under her breath.

"Thanks, Dad," Kelsey said, glaring at her mother. "I'm sure he'll love it."

Dylan came down the stairs and walked into the kitchen, carrying his suitcase.

"Did you get everything?" Kelsey's mother asked him.

"Everything but my cookies," Dylan said.

"Here they are," Mrs. North said, handing him a large package.

"Thanks, Kelly. I miss these."

"I'll send you some," she replied.

"Thanks. I'll hide them from Ian," he replied.

Tyler followed Dylan a few moments later, carrying his silver carry-on and Kelsey's bag.

"Thanks, Tyler," Kelsey said to him.

"Was that everything?" he asked her. She nodded.

"It's going to be so quiet around here," Mr. North said.

"Only for a few weeks. Then Tyler and I will be back," Kelsey said.

"Coming back for Christmas, Olsen?" Dylan said.

"Afraid so," Tyler replied.

"Looking forward to it," Mr. North said brightly.

"I'll be spending Christmas with my family," Dylan said. "I missed it last year."

"Have a nice time," Tyler said. Dylan kissed Mrs. North on the cheek.

"Miss you," she said sadly.

"I'll be back," Dylan said, looking at Tyler.

Tyler and Kelsey spent the entire car ride talking about the vacation events. Kelsey was happy that it had ended as well as it did.

They left Tyler's car and went upstairs once they were on the ferry. They stood outside and watched the waves as the ferry cut across Puget Sound. When it got too windy, they retreated inside to the seats. It was noisy as kids ran around, and families chatted, heading back to the city after the long weekend.

Kelsey glanced out of the ferry window at the Seattle skyline. They were almost back to Seattle.

"So, Kels," Tyler began, then his phone beeped with a message. "Hang on, sorry," he said, retrieving his phone and looking at the message. He shook his head and chuckled.

"What is it?" Kelsey asked him.

"Nothing," he said, pocketing the phone. "I have to go to Medina after I drop you at school. Anyway," he began again, but suddenly an announcement came over the loudspeaker.

"We are now approaching the Seattle ferry dock. Please return to your cars. Thank you."

Tyler sighed. "Let's go," he said, standing up. Kelsey joined him and they walked toward the stairs.

"What did you want to say?" Kelsey asked him.

"It doesn't matter, I'll tell you at the gym tomorrow morning," Tyler replied.

After saying goodbye to Tyler, who headed right back to his car after carrying Kelsey's bag to her apartment, Kelsey hung out in her room until Jessica arrived around 10 p.m.

"Hey, Kels!" Jessica said, wheeling her bag into the apartment.

"Welcome back," Kelsey said coming out into the living room and giving Jessica a hug.

"So Ryan lived?" Kelsey asked as she followed her into Jessica's bedroom.

Jessica was thoughtful as she unzipped her bag. "It was touch and go for a while, but he pulled through."

"What happened?"

Jessica sat on her bed and shook her head. "So they pick us up at the airport, and I can already tell that it isn't going to be a good visit. My parents were acting weird from the start. They drove us to this Italian restaurant for a late dinner, and we've barely sat down before they start grilling Ryan."

"Uh, oh," Kelsey said.

"It turns out that ever since the articles came out, the staff at their office has been educating my parents about Ryan's past misdeeds. And there's so many," Jessica sighed. "They started down the list. The crashed yacht at Ibiza. The stolen plane..."

"Stolen plane?"

"Don't ask. By dessert, I wondered how Ryan's lawyers managed to keep it all straight. Then of course, my father pulled out the big gun."

"Which was?"

"Have you ever been convicted of possession of a controlled substance?

Really, my father should have been a lawyer."

"What did Ryan say?" Kelsey asked.

"He admitted it. Why lie? It's public record. He did point out that he wasn't actually the one in possession. The supermodel in his car was. It was awful. I mean, I knew all of this stuff, but it didn't occur to me that my parents would. My father, who at this point was ready to throw Ryan into the Hudson River, asked Ryan to explain himself." Jessica sighed.

She continued, "Ryan said, 'I can't change the past, but I really love Jess, and I'm trying to be a better man for her.'"

"Honestly, Kels, I wasn't sure that they were going to let him into our house. But we Hunters are courteous people, and they had told me to invite him, so it was clear we would all suffer together over the weekend."

Jessica continued, "We went home and got settled in. Ryan and I sat in the living room with my parents, watching TV and my parents kept glancing over, as if Ryan was on the F.B.I.'s most wanted list. And then Ryan turned it all around. He asked me if I was cold."

"What?"

"He asked me if I was cold. I was, you know, my parents don't like to turn up the heat. So I said yes, and Ryan jumped up and left the room. When he came back, he was carrying his Darrow sweatshirt and a pair of socks. He handed me the sweatshirt, and put the socks on my feet."

"Really?"

"It was so sweet. And it was like a light flipped on in the room for my parents. After a month of being convinced that Ryan was some rich boy delinquent out to corrupt their daughter, they realized that maybe he did really care about me, and was committed to changing. So they gave him a chance over the next few days."

"It was slow going, I mean there was so much baggage. But at the airport today, my dad shook Ryan's hand and told him to take care of himself. And they didn't tell me to stop seeing him."

"Awesome, Jess."

"Yeah, I can breathe again," Jessica said. "I'm not sure what's gotten into them. They did tell me to bring him back at Christmas. Joey and Andrea were at her parents' house this year, so Ryan didn't meet them."

First thing Monday morning, Kelsey went to the gym to work out. Per usual, it was silent when she entered. Kelsey started her morning run, expecting Tyler to come into the gym within ten minutes of her arrival. But when she got off the treadmill and began working out with weights, he still hadn't arrived. Kelsey finished her workout and headed back to her apartment floor.

She decided to knock on Tyler's door and see if he was back. It wasn't like the diligent Mr. Olsen not to go to the gym after he said he would be there. She opened the door of the boys' apartment with her key, and Kelsey walked to Tyler's door and knocked.

She heard movement in the room, and the door opened, but to Kelsey's surprise, it wasn't opened by Tyler. A tired but beautiful girl with long blonde hair peered out at her. She was wearing a man's white shirt, which she had wrapped around her otherwise naked body.

Kelsey involuntarily glanced at the cuffs. Ryan and Zachary's shirts were always monogrammed, Tyler's were not. The cuff was blank.

"Yes?" the girl asked sleepily.

"Sorry," Kelsey said. "I was looking for Tyler."

"Tyler's still asleep," the girl said, yawning.

"Oh, okay. Sorry," Kelsey said. She turned away from the door and the girl closed the door behind her.

Kelsey found herself involuntarily turning back to the closed door. As she stood silently, her heart breaking into a thousand pieces, she felt a tear roll down her cheek.

Want my unreleased 5000-word story
Introducing the Billionaire Boys Club
and other free gifts from time to time?

Then join my mailing list at

http://www.caramillerbooks.com/inner-circle/

Subscribe now and read it now!

You can also follow me on Twitter and Facebook

Printed in Great Britain
by Amazon